"Etgar Keret is the voice of young Israel . . . [His] stories . . . deal with all the important things, friendship, sadness, fear . . . Unlike anything else the country [is] producing."

—LINDA GRANT, *The Independent*

"Keret's short stories are filled with antiheroes. There are no brave Maccabees, no swashbuckling warriors. Instead, his sketches dramatize the mundane details of daily life . . . Keret's [stories] seem to promise that there is more to life than Merkava tanks and suicide killers, more even than nanotech or IPOs. His quirky collections . . . offer a glimpse into the Israeli subconscious. They satisfy jumbled, humble hopes."

—KEVIN PERAINO, *Newsweek*

"Exhilarating . . . You set out initially in a straightforward direction, and then just as you're finding your stride, it's as though the pavement drops and suddenly you start falling. Whoa! Oops! Bang!"

—IAM SANSOM, *The Guardian*

"His enchantingly witty stories suggest that a keen intelligence can still flourish even when the air is full of flying metal . . . Our best chance is that Etgar Keret will become a craze, a craze for sanity."

—CLIVE JAMES

"In a country where 'Bulldozer' is one of the prime minister's nicknames, and where the model writer, for decades, has been the strapping kibbutznik and war veteran Amos Oz, Keret writes from some other Israel, populated by weak, confused nobodies. And yet Keret is not just widely read, he is absorbed, above all by the young."

—NANCY UPDIKE, *The New York Times Magazine*

Lihi Lapid

ETGAR KERET

THE NIMROD FLIPOUT

Etgar Keret is the author of three bestselling story collections, one novella, three graphic novels, and a children's book. His fiction has been translated into more than twenty languages and has been the basis for more than forty short films. He lives and teaches in Tel Aviv.

THE NIMROD FLIPOUT

ETGAR KERET

Translated from the Hebrew by
Miriam Shlesinger and Sondra Silverston

FARRAR, STRAUS AND GIROUX • NEW YORK

FARRAR, STRAUS AND GIROUX
19 Union Square West, New York 10003

"Fatso," "The Nimrod Flipout," "Shooting Tuvia," "Your Man," "Eight Percent
of Nothing," "Surprise Egg," "Actually, I've Had Some Phenomenal Hard-ons
Lately," "More Life," "Glittery Eyes," "Malffunction," "For Only 9.99 (Inc. Tax
and Postage)," "Angle," and "Himme" were translated by Miriam Shlesinger.

"One Kiss on the Mouth in Mombasa," "Shriki," "Pride and Joy," "Dirt," "Teddy
Trunk," "Halibut," "Horsie," "My Girlfriend's Naked," "Bottle," "A Visit to the
Cockpit," "A Thought in the Shape of a Story," "Gur's Theory of Boredom,"
"The Tits on an Eighteen-Year-Old," "Bwoken," "Baby," "Ironclad Rules,"
and "A Good-Looking Couple" were translated by Sondra Silverston.

Library of Congress Cataloging-in-Publication Data
Keret, Etgar, 1967–
    The Nimrod flipout / Etgar Keret ; translated from the Hebrew by
Miriam Shlesinger and Sondra Silverston.— 1st American ed.
        p.   cm.
    ISBN-13: 978-0-374-22243-7 (pbk. : alk. paper)
    ISBN-10: 0-374-22243-6 (pbk. : alk. paper)
    I. Shlesinger, Miriam, 1947–   II. Silverston, Sondra.   III. Title.

PJ5054.K375N56 2006
892.4'36—dc22

                                                        2005051141

Designed by Gretchen Achilles

www.fsgbooks.com

1   3   5   7   9   10   8   6   4   2

CONTENTS

THE NIMROD
FLIPOUT

FATSO

Surprised? Of course I was surprised. You go out with a girl. First date, second date, a restaurant here, a movie there, always just matinees. You start sleeping together, the sex is mind-blowing, and pretty soon there's feeling too. And then, one day, she shows up in tears, and you hug her and tell her to take it easy, everything's going to be OK, and she says she can't stand it anymore, she has this secret, not just a secret, something really awful, a curse, something she's been wanting to tell you from the beginning but she didn't have the guts. This thing, it's been weighing her down, and now she's got to tell you, she's simply got to, but she knows that as soon as she does, you'll leave her, and you'll be absolutely right to leave her, too. And then she starts crying all over again.

I won't leave you, you tell her. I won't. I love you. You try to look concerned, but you're not. Not really. Or rather, if you are concerned, it's about her crying, not about her secret. You know by now that these secrets that always make a woman fall to pieces are usually something along the lines of doing it with an animal, or a Mormon, or with someone who paid her for it. I'm a whore, they always wind up saying. And you hug them and say, no you're not. You're not. And if they don't stop crying all you can do is say *shhh*. It's something really terrible, she insists, as if she's picked up on how nonchalant you are about it, even though you've tried to hide it. In the pit of your stomach it may sound terrible, you tell her, but that's just acoustics. As soon as you let it out it won't seem anywhere near as bad—you'll see. And she almost believes you. She hesitates and then she asks: What if I told you that at night I turn into a heavy, hairy man, with no neck, with a gold ring on his pinkie, would you still love me? And you tell her of course you would. What else can you say? That you wouldn't? She's just trying to test you, to see whether you love her unconditionally—and you've always been a winner at tests. In fact, as soon as you say it, she melts, and you do it, right there in the living room. And afterward, you lie there holding each other tight, and she cries because she's so relieved, and you cry too. Go figure. And unlike all the other times, she doesn't get up and go. She stays there and falls asleep. And you lie awake, looking at her beautiful body, at the sunset outside, at the moon appearing as if out of nowhere, at the silvery light flickering over her body, stroking the hair on her back. And within five minutes you find yourself lying next to this guy—this short fat guy. And the guy gets up and smiles at you, and awkwardly gets dressed. He leaves the room and you follow him, spellbound. He's in the den now, his thick fingers fiddling with the remote, zapping to the sports channels. Championship soccer. When they miss a pass, he curses the TV; when they score, he gets up and does a little victory dance.

After the game he tells you that his throat is dry and his stomach is growling. He could really use a beer and a big steak. Well-done if possible, and with lots of onion rings, but he'd settle for pork chops. So you get in the car and take him to this restaurant that he knows about. This new twist has you worried, it really does, but you have no idea what you should do. Your command-

and-control centers are down. You shift gears at the exit, in a daze. He's right there beside you in the passenger seat, tapping that gold-ringed pinkie of his. At the next intersection, he rolls down his window, winks at you, and yells at a girl who's trying to thumb a ride: Hey, baby, wanna play nanny goat and ride in the back? Later, the two of you pack in the steak and the chops and the onion rings till you're about to explode, and he enjoys every bite, and laughs like a baby. And all that time you keep telling yourself it's got to be a dream. A bizarre dream, yes, but definitely one that you'll snap out of any minute.

On the way back, you ask him where he'd like you to drop him off, and he pretends not to hear you, but he looks despondent. So you wind up taking him home. It's almost three a.m. I'm hitting the sack, you tell him, and he waves his hand, and stays in the beanbag chair, staring at the fashion channel. You wake up the next morning, exhausted, and your stomach hurts. And there she is, in the living room, still dozing. But by the time you've had your shower, she's up. She gives you a sheepish hug, and you're too embarrassed to say anything. Time goes by and you're still together. The sex just gets better and better. She's not so young anymore, and neither are you, and suddenly you find yourselves talking about a baby. And at night, you and fatso hit the town like you've never done in your life. He takes you to restaurants and bars you didn't even know existed, and you dance on the tables together, and break plates like there's no tomorrow. He's really nice, the fatso, a little crass, especially with women; sometimes the things he comes out with make you want to sink into the floor. Other than that, he's lots of fun. When you first met him, you didn't give a damn about soccer, but now you know every team. And whenever one of your favorites wins, you feel like you've made a wish and it's come true. Which is a pretty exceptional feeling for someone like you, who hardly knows what he wants most of the time. And so it goes: every night you fall asleep with him struggling to stay awake for the Argentinean finals, and in the morning there she is, the beautiful, forgiving woman who you love, too, till it hurts.

THE NIMROD FLIPOUT

MIRON FREAKS OUT

When it comes to Miron's problem, there are, as they say, several schools of thought. The doctors think it's some trauma he suffered when he was in the army that resurfaced all of a sudden in his brain, like a turd that comes floating back at you in the toilet long after you've flushed. His parents are convinced it's all because of the mushrooms he ate in the East, which turned his brain to quiche. The guy who found him there and brought him back to Israel says it's because of this Dutch girl he met in Dharamsala, who broke his heart. And Miron himself says it's God who's messing with his mind. Tapping into his brain like a bat, telling it one thing, then the opposite, anything, just to pick a fight. According to Miron, after He created the world, God pretty much rested on His laurels for a couple of million years. Until Miron came along all of a sudden, and started asking questions, and God broke out in a sweat. Because God could tell straight off that unlike the rest of humanity, Miron was nobody's chump. As soon as you gave him the smallest opening, he'd slam right through it, and God—as everyone knows—is really big on dishing it out, but not on taking it, and the last thing He feels like putting up with is a rebuttal, especially from a guy like Miron, and from the minute He realized what was going on, He just kept driving Miron around the bend, hassling him whenever He could, with everything from bad dreams to girls who wouldn't put out. Anything to make him fall apart.

The doctors asked Uzi and me to help them a little with Miron's case history, because the three of us have known each other all our lives. They asked us all kinds of questions about the army, about what had happened with Nimrod. But most of it we couldn't remember, and even the little bit that we did remember we didn't tell them because the truth was that they didn't exactly look like nice guys, and Miron had told us a couple of things that bordered on something you'd see on *60 Minutes*. After that, during visiting hours, Miron begged us to bring him some hummus from the hunchback, because more than anything else, it was the food here that was doing him in. "It's been three weeks since I got here," he figured, "and if you add that to the four months in the East, that's almost six months without hummus. I wouldn't wish that on my worst enemy, I really wouldn't." So we went to get him some. The hunchback said he didn't do takeout. "Only sit-down," he snarled, half-menacing, half-indifferent, the way he does. "I'm not running a snack bar here." So we ordered a plate of hummus, and stuck it in the pita ourselves. When we got back, Miron's mother was there. She said hi to Uzi, but not to me. She hasn't spoken to me for years, on account of me influencing her son to experiment with drugs. We didn't give him the hummus while she was still there, because we were afraid she'd tell the doctors. So we waited for her to leave. Meanwhile, the *ful* was getting cold, but that didn't matter to Miron, who wolfed it down. Three days later they discharged him. The doctors said his reaction to the medications was remarkable. Miron still insists it was on account of the hummus.

UZI LOSES IT

In June, Miron and I went down to Sinai. Uzi was supposed to come too, but he stood us up at the last second for an appointment with some dot-com German from Düsseldorf who could put up millions for a project with Uzi's company. It was supposed to be a kind of celebration, in honor of the fact that Miron wasn't considered crazy anymore, and Uzi felt kind of embarrassed about his childish attraction to money, so he promised that as soon as his appointment was over he'd join us there. "I'll bet you anything he doesn't show," Miron said. "A double bet: First off, he won't show, and second, give him three more months and he'll marry the Turnip." I didn't want to bet Miron about either, because what he said sounded depressing but basically true. Turnip was our code name for Uzi's obnoxious girlfriend who was also deep into all those virtual hi-tech deals that Uzi loved to manage. I remember him asking us once why we called her Turnip, and Miron told him something about how it was because turnips are underrated: some people don't realize how good they can be. Uzi didn't really buy it, but he never asked about it again.

If life is one big party, Sinai is definitely the chill-out room. And even Miron and I, who hardly did anything in regular life anyway, could appreciate the ultimate nothingness of the place. Everywhere you looked on our beach, you saw dozens of spaced-out hippie chicks, and Miron kept hitting on them, going on about all the time he'd spent in the East. It even worked, sometimes. Me, I didn't have the energy, or the coordination either. So I just smoked lots of weed, stared at the sea, and kept debating whether to order a pineapple pancake for lunch or take my chances with the fish. I also kept an eye on Miron from a distance, checking to see if he'd really straightened out. He still came up with some pretty weird stuff, like for instance when he insisted on taking a shit right near our hut because he was too lazy to walk all the way to the restaurant. But the truth is that he used to do stuff like that before he went crazy too.

"I have a good feeling about that short one with the navel stud," he told me at night after we came back from the restaurant on the beach. "You have to admit, she's cute, isn't she?" The two of us were sitting around, out of it, just staring out at the sea. "Listen," I told him, "about that whole thing when they put you away, I know Uzi and me acted like it was no big thing, but you scared the shit out of us." Miron just shrugged. "It was pretty freaky, like suddenly I started hearing voices—talking, singing. Like some broken radio that you can't figure out how to turn off. It drives you up the wall. You can't think straight even for a second. I'm telling you, I felt as if someone was trying to flip me out. And then it just stopped." Miron took one more drag on the cigarette, and put it out in the sand. "And I'll tell you something else," he said. "I know this sounds wacked, but I think it was Nimrod."

The next day, contrary to all our predictions, Uzi arrived. Too bad I didn't take Miron up on his bet. As soon as Uzi put his bag down in the hut he dragged us straight to the restaurant, chewed some squid, and told us all about how the German guy had turned out to be even more of a pushover than he'd expected, and how happy he was to be with us, with his best friends, in Sinai, his favorite place in the whole world. After that, he went charging up and down the beach, calling "Yo Bro" at anything that moved, and hugging every Bedouin or Egyptian who wasn't fast enough to get away. When he got tired of that too, Uzi made us play backgammon with him, and after he beat both of us, he clobbered one of the Bedouins too, and then he made the Bedouin traipse up and down the beach behind his bald opponent yelling, "Watch out, girls, Abu-Gara's big." Miron tried to chill him out with a joint, but that only made Uzi crazier. He started coming on strong to a forty-year-old American tourist, gave up in no time, ate three pancakes, told Miron and me that he couldn't get over the peace and quiet of the place, ordered kebab, and suggested that maybe the three of us and his new Bedouin friend, who turned out to be a taxi driver, could go down to play the casino at Taba. Miron was dead set against it, because he figured he was just about to get lucky with navel stud, but Uzi was so worked up that he didn't stand a chance. "No shit," Miron said as soon as we got into the taxi. "The guy's completely lost it."

Abu-Gara and the Bedouin made a killing at Taba, swooping down on one table after the next, leaving nothing behind them but shattered croupiers and scorched earth. Between killings, Uzi wolfed down enormous slabs of apple pie and chocolate mousse cake. Miron and me just sat there, watching patiently, waiting for him to wear himself out. But the thing was, he just kept getting stronger and stronger. Once Uzi and the Bedouin had finished humiliating the casino and divvying up their winnings, we took the taxi to the border station. Miron and me reminded Uzi that we were supposed to be heading back, but he said it was out of the question. As far as he was concerned, the day was still young, and there was no reason not to cash in at a couple of clubs in Eilat before heading back. He made sure to give the Bedouin his business card, and they kissed about eighty times. Miron made one more try to persuade the Bedouin to take us back to the beach, leaving Uzi to continue his escapades on his own, but the Bedouin told us off and insisted that for us to leave a wonderful friend like Abu-Gara right in the middle of a celebration would be a disgrace, and he'd have loved to come with us himself except he wasn't allowed to cross the border. After that he kissed us too, got into the taxi, and disappeared. When Uzi got tired of the Spiral, we went to the Yacht Pub and then to some hotel called the Blue Something, and only then, after Miron and I had refused two different times to let him get some call girls sent up to our room, Uzi turned over on his stomach and started to snore.

Ever since that time in Sinai, Uzi's company's been on a roll. After the German pushover, Uzi found two other suckers, one an American and the other from India, and it looked like he was about to knock the whole world on its ass. Miron said it only went to show how crazy all those businesspeople were. Because the fact was that ever since Uzi'd gone off the deep end, he'd been getting bigger and bigger. Sometimes we'd still try to drag him with us to the beach or the pool hall, but even when he did come, he was so busy the whole time telling everyone how much he was enjoying it and what a great time we were having together, and checking the voice mail on his cell phone, that after an hour with him you'd simply lose the desire to live. "Don't worry. He'll outgrow it," I'd try to tell Miron, as Uzi got caught up in another transatlantic call just when it was his turn to shoot. "Sure," Miron would say in the tone of an ex-wacko who's got it all figured out, "and if it's doing the rounds, you're next."

NEXT IN LINE TO LOSE HIS SHIT

The next morning, I woke up in an utter panic. I had no idea what was causing it. I lay there, pressing my back to the mattress, trying not to move till I could figure out what had me so scared. But the more time went by, the less I could figure out what brought it on, and the more scared I got. I lie there in bed frozen, and keep telling myself, in the second person, as calmly as I can, "Take it easy, man, take it easy. This isn't really happening, it's all in your head." But the thought that this thing, whatever it is, is inside my head makes it a thousand times more horrifying. I decide to tell myself who I am, to say my name a few times in a row.

That's bound to help me get a grip on myself. Except that all of a sudden even my name is gone. At least that gets me out of bed. I crawl around the house, searching for bills, mail, anything with my name written on it. I open the front door and look at the other side of it, where there's an orange sticker with the inscription: "Have a hell of a life!" In the hallway there's the loud laughter of kids and the sound of footsteps approaching. I close the door and lean against it. Stay cool. In a minute I'll remember, or not—maybe I never had a name. Whatever happens, that isn't why I'm sweating so hard that my pulse is about to blow my brains out, that's not it, it's something else. "Take it easy," I whisper to myself again. "Take it easy, whatever your name is. This can't go on much longer, it'll be over soon."

As soon as it eased up, I phoned Uzi and Miron, and arranged to meet them both at the beach. It was just a few hundred yards from my place, and I had no problem remembering how to get there, except that all the streets suddenly looked different, and I had to keep stopping to check the signs to make sure they were really the right ones. Not just the streets, everything looked different, even the sky was kind of squashed, and low.

"I told you your turn would come," Miron says, and sucks at the red tip of his Wave-on-a-Stick Popsicle. "First I lost it, then Uzi." "I didn't lose it," Uzi protested. "I was just a little high, that's all." "Whatever," Miron went on. "It's your turn now." "Ron isn't losing it either," Uzi said, beginning to get worked up. "Why do you keep putting those ideas in his head?" "Ron?" I ask. "Is that my name?" "Know what?" Uzi concedes. "Maybe he has lost it a little. Can I get a bite?" Miron hands him the Popsicle, knowing perfectly well he'll never see it again. "Tell me," he asks. "When it started, didn't you feel there was someone in your head?" "I don't know." I hesitated. "Maybe I did." "I'm telling you," Miron whispered, as if it was a secret. "I could feel him. He was saying things that only he could know. I'm sure it was Nimrod."

NIMROD'S FLIPOUT

Until he turned twelve, Nimrod was a shitty person. The kind of whiner that, if he wasn't your best friend, you'd have kicked his ass a long time ago. And then one day, just before his bar mitzvah, they put insoles in his shoes, and suddenly the guy was a whole new human being. Yes, Miron, Uzi, and I had been friends with Nimrod even before that, but now, when he became nice too, it actually started to be fun to be around him.

Later, in high school, Uzi and me were in the honors program and Miron and Nimrod went to vocational school and mostly the beach. Then came the army. Miron was drafted six months before us, and by the time our turn came he'd sucked up to enough people to make sure we'd all be in the same unit with a cushy office job. Nimrod used to call it the padded pad.

Most of the time, we didn't do anything except sit around in the canteen, threatening to file complaints against our commanders, and go home every day at five. Other than that, Uzi would surf at the Sheraton, I was forever jerking off, Miron took courses at the Open University, and Nimrod had a girlfriend. Nimrod's girlfriend was as good as they get, and because all of us except him were virgins, that made her even better. I remember I once asked Miron what he would do—hypothetically, I mean—if she came to his house, say, and asked him to fuck her. And Miron said he didn't know, but whatever he did, he'd regret it the rest of his life. Which is a nice answer but knowing him, he'd be sure to take the fucking option first and the regretting option second.

But with Nimrod it wasn't even that he was horny; he was simply in love with her. Her name was Netta, which is a name

that I still love to this day, and she was a paramedic at the infirmary. Nimrod told me once that he could lie next to her in bed for
hours without getting bored, and that the place he liked her to
touch the most was the spot on his foot where everyone had an
arch but his was flat.

At the base we would do guard duty twice a month, and once
every two months we had to stay the weekend, which Nimrod always managed to arrange for days when Netta had infirmary
duty so that even on guard duty they were together. A year and a
half later, she left him. It was a strange kind of split, even she
couldn't really explain why it happened, and after that Nimrod
didn't care when his guard duty came out. One Saturday, Miron,
Nimrod, and I were on duty together. Uzi had just managed to
forge some kind of a medical pass for himself. We were all on the
same patrol—Miron first, Nimrod second, and me third. And
even before I had a chance to replace him, this officer rushed in
and said that the guy on duty had put a bullet in his head.

ROUND TWO

The second time Miron lost it, it was much more unpleasant. We
didn't say a word about it to his parents, and I just moved in with
him till it passed. Most of the time he kept quiet, sitting in the
corner and writing a kind of book to himself, which was supposed
to eventually replace the Bible. Sometimes, when we'd run out of
beer or cigarettes, he would swear at me a little, with conviction,
and say that I was really a demon disguised as a friend, and I'd
been sent to torment him. Other than that, he was almost bear-
able. Uzi, on the other hand, took his extended period of sanity
very hard. He didn't admit it, but it seemed like he'd really had it
with that skyrocketing international company of his. Somehow,
whenever he flipped, he had a lot more energy to write all these

grim prospectuses and things and go to boring meetings. Now that he was a little more sane, the whole businessman thing was that much harder to handle. Even though it seemed as if his company was about to go public and he'd be sitting back, raking in a couple of million. Me, I'd been fired from another job, and Miron, in a lucid moment when he was off beer and cheap cigarettes, said that he was the one who'd gotten me fired with his unearthly spiritual powers. I don't know, maybe all those jobs just aren't for me, and all I should really do is sit it out till Uzi strikes it rich and tosses me a little.

The second time Uzi started going batshit proved once and for all that there was definitely a rotation thing going on, and I started to worry because I knew I was next. Miron, who'd chilled out by then, kept insisting it had something to do with Nimrod. "I don't know what he wants exactly. Maybe he wants us to even the score or something. But one thing's for sure, so long as we don't do it—whatever it is—I don't think it's going to stop." "Even what score?" I countered. "Nimrod killed himself." "How do you know?" Miron wouldn't let it go that easily. "Maybe he was murdered. Besides, maybe it isn't exactly vengeance. Maybe it's just something he wants us to do so he can rest in peace. Like in those horror films, you know, where they open a bar on an ancient burial ground, and as long as it stays there, the ghosts can't rest in peace." In the end, we decided that Miron and I would go to the Kiryat Shaul cemetery to make sure nobody had set up a Coke-and-mineral-water stand on Nimrod's grave by mistake. The only reason I agreed to go there with him was that I was freaking out about it being my turn soon. The truth was that of the three of us, my crack-up was the worst.

Nimrod's grave had stayed exactly the same. We hadn't been there in six years. At first, on Memorial Day for the fallen soldiers, his mother still used to call us. But with all those military rabbis and those aunts who'd faint away again every year, we weren't exactly eager to go. We kept telling ourselves that we'd go some other day, on our own special memorial day, except we always put it off. Last time we talked about it, Uzi said that actually every time we went to shoot pool together or took in a movie or a pub or whatever, it was a commemoration of Nimrod too, because when the three of us are together, then even if we're not exactly thinking about him, he's there.

It took Miron and me maybe an hour to find the grave, which actually seemed to be well tended and clean, with a couple of stones on top as proof that someone had been there not too long before. I looked at the dates on the grave and thought about how I was just about to turn thirty, and Nimrod wasn't even nineteen yet. It was kind of weird, because somehow, whenever I thought about him he was sort of my age, when in fact I hardly had any hair left and he was not much more than a kid. On our way out, we returned the cardboard yarmulkes to the box by the gate, and Miron said he didn't have any more ideas, but we could always have a séance. Outside the cemetery, on the other side of the fence, there was a fat, shaggy cat chewing a piece of meat. I looked at him, and as if he felt it, he looked up from the chunk of meat and smiled at me. It was a mean and ruthless smile, and he went back to chewing the meat without lowering his gaze. I felt the fear running through my body, from the hard part of my brain to the soft part of my bones. Miron didn't notice there was something wrong with me, and kept on talking. "Relax, Ron," I told myself. The fact that I remembered my name made me so happy tears came to my eyes. "Take a deep breath, don't fall apart. Whatever it is, it'll pass." At that very moment, in the smelly office of some attorney in Petah Tikva, Uzi was chickening out of signing a deal that would transfer thirty-three percent of his company's shares to an anonymous group of Polish investors for a million and a half bucks. Think about it, if only he'd stayed flipped out for another fifteen minutes, he could have taken us and the Turnip on a Caribbean cruise, and instead he was on his way home in a number-54 bus from Petah Tikva with an asshole driver who wouldn't even turn on the AC.

TRI-LI-LI-LI-LA

When Uzi announced he was going to marry the Turnip, we hardly even put up an argument. Somehow we'd known it would happen. Uzi lied and said it was his idea, and that it was mainly so he could take out a mortgage from the bank for an apartment that he'd planned to buy anyway someplace near Netanyah. "How can you marry her?" Miron tried to reason with him, without much conviction. "You don't even love her." "How can you say I don't love her?" Uzi protested. "We've been together for three years.

D'you know I've never cheated on her?" "That's not because you love her," Miron said. "It's just because you're uncoordinated." We were just shooting pool, and Uzi had clobbered both of us with the bull's-eye shots of someone who'd made up his mind to squeeze every drop out of the little bit of luck he still had left, quickly, before it had a chance to run out. There was only the eight ball left, and it was Uzi's turn. "Let's make a bet," I said, in an act of desperation. "If you pocket the eight ball, Miron and I will never call her Turnip again, ever. And if you miss, then you drop the whole wedding thing for a year." "When it comes to feelings, I never make bets," Uzi said, and pocketed the eight effortlessly. "Besides," he said, smiling, "it's too late. We've already printed up the invitations." "What were you thinking, betting him like that?" Miron told me off later. "That shot was a sure thing."

By the time the date rolled around, Uzi had managed to lose it two more times, and on both occasions he said he would call it all off, but changed his mind right away. As for me, I just crashed in Miron's apartment while it was going on. Now that we were wigged out most of the time, it was much nicer living together. And besides, I couldn't really afford my own place. Miron had stolen a big pile of wedding invitations from Uzi, and we would use them to make filters for joints. "How can you go and marry someone whose mother's name is Yentl?" he would ask Uzi whenever we'd smoke a joint together, and Uzi would just stare at the ceiling and give that spaced-out laugh of his. The truth was that even though I was on Miron's side on this, I could see it wasn't much of an argument.

Three days before the wedding we held a séance. We bought a piece of blue construction paper, I drew all the letters on it with a black marker, and Miron got a glass from the kitchen, one of those cheap ones. He said he'd had it for ages, from his parents' house, and that Nimrod must have used it. We turned out all the lights and placed the glass in the middle of the board. Each of us put a finger on it, and we waited. After five minutes, Uzi got tired of sitting there, and said he had to take a shit. He turned on the lights in the living room, found a week-old sports section, and locked himself in the bathroom. Miron and me rolled a joint meanwhile. I asked Miron—if it had worked, and if the glass had moved, what did he expect to happen. That pissed Miron off, and he said it was too early to say it hadn't succeeded and that just because Uzi gets bored with everything so quickly, it didn't mean that it wasn't going to work. After Uzi finally came out of the bathroom, Miron switched the lights back off and asked us both to concentrate. We put our fingers on the glass again, and waited. Nothing happened. Miron insisted that we try again, and neither of us could work up the energy to argue with him. A few minutes later, the glass began to move. Slowly at first, but within seconds it was racing all over the board. Miron left his finger on it the whole time and kept writing down with his other hand each of the letters that it stopped on. T-r-i-l-i-l-i-l-i-l-a the glass hummed, and came to a smooth stop on the exclamation mark in the right-hand corner of the board. We waited a while longer, and nothing happened. Uzi turned on the light. "Tri-li-li-li-la?" he said, annoyed. "What are we, in kindergarten or something? You moved it, Miron, so don't give me any Agent Mulder shit. Tri-li-li-li-la? Fuck it. I'm beat. I've been up since seven. I'm going to sleep at Liraz's." Liraz was the Turnip's name, and she lived close by. Miron kept staring at the board with the letters he'd drawn even after Uzi left, and for a while I read the sports supplement that Uzi had taken to the bathroom, and when I'd read it all, I told Miron I was going to crash. Miron said OK, but that first he just wanted us to give one more chance to the thing with the glass, because no matter how much he thought about it, that Tri-li-li-li-la thing didn't mean a thing to him. So we turned out the light again, and put the glass in place. This time it started moving right away, and Miron took down the letters.

D-O-N'-T-L-E-A-V-E-M-E-A-L-O-N-E the glass said, and then it stopped again.

MAZEL TOV

The wedding itself was awful, with a rabbi who thought he was a comedian and a DJ who played Enrique Iglesias and Ricky Martin. Still, Miron met this girl there with a squeaky voice but an amazing body. Plus, after the ceremony, he freaked Uzi out when he told him that the glass he'd stepped on was the one we'd used for Nimrod's séance. While this was going on, I got another of my anxiety attacks and puked about four pounds of chopped liver in the toilet.

That same night, Uzi and the Turnip flew off on their honey-

moon in the Seychelles. Me and Miron sat on the balcony drinking coffee. Miron had a new thing going now. Whenever he'd
make us coffee, he'd always make one instant for Nimrod too in
the séance glass, and he'd put it on the table, the way you leave
out a glass for Elijah on Passover, and after we were through
drinking, he'd pour it down the sink. Miron did his version of the
DJ, and I laughed. The truth was we were incredibly sad. You
could call it chauvinist, possessive, egocentric, lots of names, but
the whole wedding thing weighed us down. I asked Miron to read
me a chapter from that book of his, the one he writes whenever
he flips, and is supposed to replace the Bible. Actually, I'd asked
him a million times, and he'd never do it. When he's flipped he's
scared someone will steal his ideas, and when he's sane he's just
embarrassed. "Come on," I said. "Just a chapter, like a kind of
bedtime story." And Miron was so depressed that he agreed. He
pulled a bunch of his scribbled pages out of his shoe drawer. Before he started reading, he looked at me and said, "You realize it's
just the two of us left now, don't you? I mean, Uzi will still be one
of us and all, but he won't be on Nimrod's rounds." "How can you
tell?" I said, even though in my heart I'd thought of this even before he said it. "Listen," Miron said. "Even Nimrod knows it isn't
right to pick on someone who's already married. The way he flips
us out isn't always the best idea either, but the truth is that he
wouldn't be doing it to us if he didn't feel deep inside that we
agree. There's nothing we can do about it. We're screwed, Ron.
There's just me and you, one week each, like kitchen duty."

Miron picked up the pile of pages and cleared his throat, like
a radio announcer who chokes in the middle of reading the news.

"And if one of us suddenly goes?" I asked.

"Goes?" Miron looked up from his pages, confused. "Goes
where?"

"I don't know," I said, smiling. "Just goes. Imagine what if tomorrow the woman of my dreams comes on to me in the street, and we fall in love, and I marry her. Then you'd be the only one left to flip with Nimrod, full-time, alone."

"Right." Miron gulped down the last drops of his coffee. "Good thing you're so ugly."

SHOOTING TUVIA

To Shmulik

I got Tuvia for my ninth birthday from Raanan Zagoori, who was probably the cheapest kid in the whole class. He lucked out, and his dog had puppies right on the day of my party. There were four of them, and his uncle was going to dump them all in the river, so Raanan, who only cared about how to not spend anything on the class gift, took one of them and gave it to me. The puppy was tiny, with a bark that sounded more like a wheeze, but if anyone got on his case, he'd give a deep, low kind of growl that didn't sound anything like a puppy, and it was funny, like he was impersonating some other dog. Which is why I decided to name him Tuvia, after Tuvia Tsafir, the impressionist on TV.

From Day One, my dad couldn't stand the sight of him. Tuvia didn't care much for Dad either. The truth is, Tuvia didn't much like anyone, except for me. Right from the beginning, even when he was just a little runt, he'd bark at everyone. And when he got a little bigger, he would snap at anyone who came too close. Even Mickey, who isn't the kind of guy who ever talks trash about anyone, said my dog was messed up. He never snapped or did anything bad to me though. He'd just keep jumping on me and licking me, and whenever I'd move away from him he'd start whining. Mickey said it didn't mean anything, because I was the one who fed him. But I've met lots of dogs who bark even at the people who feed them, and I knew that what Tuvia and I had going on between us wasn't about food, and that he really did like me. He just did. For no reason. Go figure out a dog. But it was something strong. The fact is, my sister fed him too, but he hated her like hell.

In the morning, when I'd go to school, he'd want to come with me, but I'd make him stay behind because I was afraid he'd make a lot of noise. We had a chain-link fence around our yard. And sometimes, when I'd come home, I'd catch Tuvia barking at some poor slob who'd had the nerve to walk down our street. Tuvia would get so mad that he'd smash right into the fence. But the second he spotted me, he always melted. Right away, he'd start crawling on the ground, wagging his tail and barking about all the assholes who'd walked down our street and gotten on his nerves that day, and about how they were lucky they'd made it out of there. He'd already bitten a couple of them, but lucky for me they didn't complain, because even without that kind of thing, my dad was watching Tuvia, just waiting for the chance to get rid of him.

Finally it came. Tuvia bit my sister, and they had to take her to the hospital for stitches. The minute they got home, Dad took Tuvia to the car. I didn't need long to figure out what was going to happen, and I started to cry, so Mom told Dad: "Come on, Joshua, why don't you just forget it. It's the kid's dog. Just look at how upset he is." Dad didn't say anything, just told my big brother to come with him. "I need him too," Mom tried. "He's a watchdog, against thieves." And my dad stopped short just before he got into the car, and said: "What do you need a watchdog for? Did anyone ever try to steal anything in this neighborhood? What's to steal here anyway?" They dumped Tuvia in the river, and stuck around to watch him being washed away. I know, because my big brother told me so. I didn't talk to anyone about it though, and except for the night they took him away, I didn't even cry.

Three days later, Tuvia turned up at school. I heard him barking under the window. He was incredibly dirty, and smelly too, but other than that he was just the same. I was proud of him for coming back. It proved that everything Mickey had said about his not really loving me wasn't true. Because if the thing between Tuvia and me had been just about food he wouldn't have come right back to me. It was smart of him to come straight to school, too. Because if he'd headed straight home without me, I don't know what my dad would've done. As it was, as soon as we got to the house Dad wanted to get rid of him. But Mom told him that maybe Tuvia had learned his lesson, and maybe he'd behave himself now. So I hosed him down in the yard, and Dad said that from now on he'd be on a leash all the time, and that if he pulled anything again, that would be it.

The truth is, Tuvia didn't learn a thing from what happened. He just got a little crazier. And every day, when I'd come back from school, I'd see him barking like a maniac at anyone who happened to walk by. One day, I came home and he wasn't there, and Dad wasn't there either. Mom said they'd come from the Border Patrol because they'd heard he was such a feisty animal that they wanted to recruit him, and that now Tuvia was a scout-dog who'd track down terrorists trying to sneak across the border. I pretended to believe her. That evening, when Dad came back with the car, Mom whispered something in his ear, and he shook his head. He'd driven thirty miles this time, all the way to Gedera, before he set Tuvia loose, just to make sure he wouldn't make it back. I know, because my big brother told me so. My brother also said it was because Tuvia had gotten loose that afternoon, and had managed to bite the dogcatcher.

Thirty miles is a long way, even by car, and on foot it's a thousand times more, especially for a dog, whose step is like a quarter of a human's. But three weeks later, Tuvia was back. He was there waiting for me at the school gate. He didn't even bark when he saw me, that's how exhausted he was, just wagged his tail without getting up. I brought him some water, and he must have lapped up about ten bowls. When Dad saw him, he couldn't believe it. "A curse, that's what this dog is," he told Mom, who went to get Tuvia some bones from the kitchen. That evening I let him stay in my bed. He fell asleep before me, and all night long he just whined and growled, snapping at anyone who pissed him off in his dream.

In the end it was Grandma of all people that he had to pick on. He didn't even bite her. Just jumped on her, and knocked her over. She got a bad bump on her head. Everyone helped her up. Me too. But then Mom sent me to the kitchen for a glass of water, and by the time I got back I saw Dad dragging Tuvia toward the car looking really mad. I didn't even try, and neither did Mom. We knew he had it coming. And Dad asked my brother to come along again, except that this time he told him to bring his M16. My brother was only an army cook, but they issued him a gun anyway. At first, he didn't catch on, and asked Dad what he needed a gun for. And Dad said it was to make Tuvia stop coming back.

They took him to the dump, and shot him in the head. My brother told me that Tuvia hadn't realized what was going to happen. He'd been in a good mood, and was turned on by all the cool stuff he found at the dump. And then, bang! From the second my brother told me, I hardly thought about Tuvia at all. All those other times, I couldn't get him out of my mind, and I'd keep trying to imagine where he was and what he was doing. But this time there was nothing to imagine anymore, so I tried to think about him as little as possible.

Six months later he came back. He was waiting for me in the school yard. There was something wrong with one of his legs, his left eye was closed, and his jaw looked completely paralyzed. But as soon as he saw me, he seemed really happy, like nothing had ever happened. When I got him home, Dad wasn't back from work yet, and Mom wasn't there either, but even when they showed up they didn't say a thing. And that was it. Tuvia stayed from then on. Twelve more years. Eventually he died of old age. And he never bit anyone again. Every now and then, when someone would pass by our fence on a bike, or just make some noise, you could still see him getting worked up, but somehow, just when he was about to lunge, he always ran out of steam.

ONE KISS ON THE MOUTH IN MOMBASA

For a minute, I got uptight. But she told me to take it easy, I had no reason to worry. She'd marry me, and if it was important, because of our parents, it could even be in a hall. That wasn't the point. The point was somewhere else altogether—three years ago, in Mombasa, when she and Lihi went there after the army. The two of them went by themselves because the guy she was seeing had just reenlisted. In Mombasa, they lived in the same place the whole time—some kind of guesthouse where a whole bunch of people hung out, mostly from Europe. Lihi refused to consider going anyplace else, because she'd just fallen in love with some German guy who lived in one of the cabins. She didn't mind staying either; she was pretty much enjoying the quiet. And even though that guesthouse was exploding with drugs and hormones, no one hassled her. They could probably just tell she wanted to be alone. No one—except for some Dutch guy who got there maybe a day after them and didn't leave until after she went back home. And he didn't actually hassle her either, just looked at her a lot. That didn't bother her. He seemed like an all-right guy, a little sad, but one of those sad guys who don't complain. They were in Mombasa for three months, and she never heard him say a word. Except for once, a week before they left, and even then, there was something so gentle about the way he talked to her, something so weightless, that it was as if he hadn't said anything at all. She explained to him that the timing was bad, told him about her boyfriend, who was some technical something in the air force, about how they'd known each other since high school. And he just smiled and nodded and moved back to his regular spot on the steps of the hut. He didn't speak to her anymore; all he did was keep looking. Except that actually, now that she thought about it, he did speak to her one more time, on the day she flew back, and he said the strangest thing. Something about how, between every two people in the world, there's a kiss. What he was actually trying to tell her was that he'd already been looking at her for three months and thinking about their kiss, how it would taste, how long it would last, how it would feel. And now she was leaving, and she had a boyfriend and everything, he understood, but just that kiss, he wanted to know if she would agree. It was actually very funny, the way he spoke, kind of confused, maybe because he didn't know English well, or he just wasn't much of a talker. But she said OK. And they kissed. And after that, he really didn't try anything and she came back to Israel with Lihi. Her boyfriend was at the airport in his uniform to pick her up in his army car. They moved in together too, and to spice up their sex life a little, they added some new things. They tied each other to the bed, dripped some wax, once they even tried to do it anally, which hurt like hell, and in the middle shit came out. In the end, they split up, and when she started school she met me. And now, we're going to get married. She has no problem with that.

She said I should pick the hall and the date and whatever I want, because it really doesn't matter to her. That isn't the point at all. Neither is that Dutch guy—I have nothing to be jealous of there. He's probably dead already from an overdose or else he's lying drunk on some sidewalk in Amsterdam, or he went and got a master's degree in something, which sounds even worse. In any case, it's not about him at all, it's that time in Mombasa. For three months, a person sits and looks at you, imagining a kiss.

YOUR MAN

When Abigail told me she wanted to break up, I was in shock. The cab had just pulled up at her place, and she got out on the sidewalk side, and said she didn't want me to come up, and that she didn't really want to talk about it either, and that most of all she never wanted to hear from me again, not even a Happy New Year or a birthday card. And then she slammed the cab door so hard that the driver cursed her through the window. I just sat there in the backseat, numb. If we'd had a fight or something, maybe I'd have been more prepared, but we'd had a really great evening. The movie sucked, but otherwise everything was fine. And then that monologue, out of nowhere, and the door slamming, and bam! Our whole six months together gone, just like that! "So what now?" the driver asked, looking at me in the rearview mirror. "Want me to take you home? If you've got a home, that is. To your parents' place? Friends? A massage parlor downtown? You're the boss, you're the king." I didn't know what I was going to do with myself. All I knew was it wasn't fair. After Ronit and I split up I swore I wouldn't let anyone get close enough to hurt me like that, but then Abigail came along, and everything was so wonderful, and I just don't deserve this. "You're right," the driver grunted. He'd turned off the ignition and tilted his seat back. "Why drive when it's so cozy here. Me, I don't care. The meter's running either way." And that's when they announced the address on the radio. "Nine Massada Street. Who's up?" And that address—I'd heard it before, and it had stayed in my memory as if someone had scratched it in there with a nail.

When Ronit dumped me it was the same, in a cab, the cab that was taking her to the airport, to be precise. She said it was over between us, and sure enough, I never heard from her again. I was left that way then too, stuck alone in the backseat of a cab. The driver that time went on and on, and I didn't hear a word. But that annoying address on the radio I happen to remember very clearly. "Nine Massada Street. Whose call?" And now, maybe it's just a coincidence, but still, I told the driver to go there. I had to find out what that address was all about. As we pulled up, I saw another cab drive away, and inside, in the backseat, was the silhouette of a small head, like a child's or a baby's. I paid the driver and got out.

It was a private house. I opened the gate, and walked up the path to the door. I rang the bell. It was a dumb thing to do, and I don't know what I'd have done if anyone had opened the door, or what I would have said. There was no reason for me to be there at that hour. But I was so mad I didn't care. I rang one more time, a long ring, and then I banged on the door, like in the army when we used to do door-to-door searches, but nobody came. In my head, thoughts about Abigail and Ronit began to get all mixed up with thoughts about other breakups, and everything sort of got lumped together. And this house, where nobody opened the door, was getting on my nerves. I started to circle around it, looking for a window I could look through. The place didn't have any windows, just a back door, mostly glass. I tried to see inside but everything was dark. I kept trying, but I couldn't get my eyes to adjust. It seemed as if the harder I tried, the blacker it all looked. It blew my mind, it really did. And suddenly it was as if I was see-ing myself from a distance, bending over, lifting a rock, wrapping it in my sweatshirt, and breaking the glass.

I reached in, careful not to cut myself, and opened the door. I groped for the light switch, and when I found it, the light was yellow and dim. One bulb for that whole big room. And that's exactly what the place was—an enormous room, no furniture, completely empty, except for one wall that was covered with photographs of women. Some of them were framed, some just stuck on the wall with masking tape, and I knew them all: There was Dalia, my girlfriend in the army; and Danielle—we went steady in high school; and Stephanie, a tourist who stayed; and Ronit. They were all there, and in the left-hand corner, in a deli-cate gold frame, was a picture of Abigail, smiling. I turned out the light and collapsed in the corner. My whole body was trembling all over. I didn't know the guy who was living here, why he was doing this to me, or how he always succeeded in wrecking things. But suddenly it all fell into place, all those breakups, all that jumping ship out of the blue—Danielle, Abigail, Ronit. It was never about us, it was always him.

I don't know how much time went by before he came home. First I heard the cab pulling away, then the sound of his key in the front door, and then the light came back on, and there he was, standing right in front of me and smiling, the son of a bitch, just looking at me and smiling. He was short, like a kid, with big eyes, no lashes, and he was holding a colored plastic schoolbag. When I got up out of my corner he just gave a weird little laugh, like he'd been caught red-handed, and asked how I'd gotten there. "So she left too, huh?" he said when I'd gotten closer. "Never mind, there'll always be another one." And me, instead of an-swering, I slammed the rock down on his head, and when he

dropped I didn't stop. I don't want another one. I want Abigail,
I want him to stop laughing. And the whole time I was bashing
him with the rock he just kept whimpering: "What're you doing,
what're you doing, what're you doing, I'm your man, your man,"
till he stopped. When it was over, I threw up. And when I'd finished throwing up, I felt lighter sort of, like on army hikes when
it's someone else's turn to take the stretcher from you, and suddenly you feel light—lighter than you'd ever thought was possible.
Light as a child. And all the hatred and the guilt and the fear that
I'd be caught—it all just disappeared.

Behind the house, not far away, were some woods, and that's
where I dumped him. The rock and the sweatshirt, which were
soaked with blood, I buried in the yard. In the weeks after that, I
kept looking for him in the papers, both in the news and in the
missing persons ads, but there was nothing. Abigail didn't answer
my messages, and someone at work told me they'd seen her in
town with this tall guy with a ponytail. I was broken up when I
heard that, but I knew there was nothing I could do. It was over
for good. A little while later, I started going out with Mia. From
the very beginning, everything with her was so *sane*. So OK. And
unlike the way I usually am with girls, with her I was very open
right from the start and all my defenses came right down. At night
I'd dream sometimes about that dwarf, how I got rid of his body
in the woods, and I'd wake up in a panic, but then I'd remind myself there was no reason to worry, he wasn't around anymore,
and then I'd hold Mia and go back to sleep.

Mia and I broke up in a cab. She told me I had no feelings, she
said I was clueless, that sometimes she'd be suffering in the worst
way, and I'd be sure she was having a good time, just because I
was. She said things had been wrong between us for a long time,
but that I hadn't even noticed. And then she started to cry. I tried
to take her in my arms, but she pulled away and said that if I

cared about her I should just let her go. I didn't know if I should go after her and keep trying. On the cab radio they gave an address: "Four Adler Road." I told the driver to take me there. Another cab was already idling there when we arrived. A couple got in, about my age, maybe a little younger. Their driver said something and they both laughed. I kept going, to Nine Massada Street. I looked for his body in the woods, but it wasn't there. The only thing I could find was a rusty iron rod. I picked it up and started walking toward the house.

The house looked just the same, dark, with the broken pane in the back door. I reached inside, groped for the handle, careful not to get cut. I found the light switch right away. The house was still empty except for the pictures on the wall, the dwarf's ugly schoolbag, and a dark, sticky stain on the floor. I studied the pictures. They were all there, in exactly the same order. When I was through with the pictures, I opened the bag and looked inside. There was some cash, a used bus pass, an eyeglass case, and a picture of Mia. In it, her hair was up, and she was looking sort of lonely. And suddenly I understood what he'd said back then, before he died, about there always being another one. I tried to picture him on the night Abigail and I broke up, going wherever it was he went, returning with the picture, making sure, I don't know how, that Mia and I would cross paths. Except I'd managed to blow it all over again. And now it wasn't so sure I'd ever meet another one. Because my man was dead and I was the one who'd killed him.

SHRIKI

Meet Reuven Shriki. A fantastic guy. The man with the plan. Someone who had the guts to live the dreams most of us don't even dare to dream. Shriki's rolling in money, but that's not the point. He also has a girlfriend, a French model, who posed in the nude for the world's best slick magazine—if you didn't jerk off to it, that was just because you couldn't get your hands on it—but that's not what makes him the man either. What's special about Shriki is that, unlike others who made it big, he's no smarter than you, no better looking, no better connected or shrewder, he isn't even luckier than you. Shriki is exactly—I mean exactly—like me and you, in every way. And that's what makes you so jealous—how did someone like *us* get so far? And anyone who tries to say it was the timing or the odds is full of crap. Shriki's secret is much simpler: he made it because he took his ordinariness as far as it could go. Instead of denying it or trying to hide it, Shriki said to himself, This is who I am, and that's all there is to it. He didn't try to make himself more or less than he was, he just flowed with it, *naturel*. He invented ordinary things, and I stress, ordinary. Not brilliant, ordinary, and that's exactly what humanity needs. Brilliant inventions might be good for brilliant people, but how many brilliant people are there in the world? Ordinary inventions, on the other hand, are good for everyone.

One day, Shriki was sitting in his living room eating olives filled with pimentos. He didn't find the filled olives very fulfilling. He liked the olives themselves much more than the pimento filling, but, on the other hand, he preferred the pimento to the original hard, bitter pit. And that's how it came to him—the first in a series of ideas that would change his life and ours—olive-filled olives, what could be simpler? An olive without a pit, filled with another olive. It took the idea a little while to catch on, but when it did, it refused to let go, like a pit bull clamping its jaws on its victim's ankle. And right after the olive-filled olives came avocado-filled avocados, and finally, the sweet crowning glory, apricot-filled apricots. In less than six years, the word "pit" lost one of its meanings. And Shriki, of course, became a millionaire. After he cleaned up in the food business, Shriki moved on to real estate, and with no special vision there either. He just made sure to buy where it was expensive, and guess what, within a year or two, it got even more expensive. That's how Shriki's assets grew and in time, he found himself investing in almost everything, except tech, a field that put him off for reasons so primal he couldn't even express them in words.

As it does with every ordinary person, money changed Shriki. He got more cheeky, more cheery, more beefy, more touchy-feely, in short, more everything. People didn't adore him, but they didn't abhor him either, which is nothing to sneeze at. Once, during a TV interview that got a little bit too personal, the interviewer asked Shriki whether he thought a lot of people aspired to be like him. "They don't have to aspire," Shriki said, smiling, half at the interviewer, half to himself. "They already are like me." And the studio filled with the sound of wild applause booming from the special electronic device the show's producers had purchased especially for up-front answers just like that one.

Imagine Shriki sitting in an armchair on the deck of his private pool, trailing a piece of pita through a plate of hummus, drinking a glass of freshly squeezed fruit juice, as his curvy girlfriend sunbathes naked on an air mattress. And now try to imagine yourselves in his place, sipping the freshly squeezed juice, tossing some sweet nothing to the naked French girl. A snap, right? And now try to imagine Shriki in your place, exactly where you are, reading this story, thinking about you there in his mansion, imagining himself sitting beside the pool in your place, and zap! Here you are again reading a story, and he's back there. Ordinary as hell, or as his French girlfriend likes to say, *trés naturel*, eating another olive and not even spitting out the pit, because there is none.

EIGHT PERCENT OF NOTHING

Benny Brokerage had been waiting for them in the doorway for almost half an hour, and when they arrived he tried to act as if it didn't make him mad. "It's all her fault," the older man said, sniggering, and held out his hand for a firm, no-nonsense shake. "Don't believe Butchie," the peroxide urged him. She looked at least fifteen years younger than her man. "We got here earlier, except we couldn't find any parking." And Benny Brokerage gave her his foxy smile, like he really gave a shit why she and Butchie were late. He showed them the apartment, which was almost completely furnished, with a high ceiling and a kitchen window that almost gave you a view of the sea. He'd barely gotten through half the usual round, when Butchie pulled out his checkbook and said he'd take it, and that he was even OK with paying a year's rent up front, except that he wanted a little bit off the top, just so he could feel like he wasn't being taken for a ride. Benny Brokerage explained that the owner was living abroad, so he wasn't at liberty to lower the price. Butchie insisted it was small change. "As far as I'm concerned," he said, "you can take it off your commission. What's your cut?" "Eight," Benny Brokerage said after a moment's pause, preferring not to risk a lie. "So you'll still be left with five," Butchie announced, and finished writing out the check. When he saw that the broker wasn't holding out his hand to take it, he added, "Look at it this way, the market's gone through the floor, and five percent of something is a lot more than eight percent of nothing."

Butchie, or Tuvia Minster, which was the name that appeared on the check, said the peroxide would drop by the next morning to pick up an extra key. Benny Brokerage said no problem, except it had to be before eleven, because he had some appointments after that. The next day, she didn't show. It was already eleven-twenty, and Benny Brokerage, who was aching to leave but didn't really want to stand her up, pulled the check out of the drawer. It had the office phone numbers, but he preferred to avoid another tedious conversation with Butchie, and went for the home number instead. It wasn't until she answered that he remembered he didn't even know her name, so he opted for "Mrs. Minster." On the phone, she somehow sounded a little less dumb, but still she couldn't remember who he was or that they'd made an appointment for that morning. Benny Brokerage kept his cool, and reminded her slowly, the way you do when you're talking to a child, how he had met with her and her husband the day before, and how they'd signed for the apartment. There was no response on the other end and when she finally asked him to describe what she looked like, he realized he'd really blown it. "The truth is," he crooned, "I must have the wrong number. What did you say your husband's name was? That's it then. I was looking for Nissim and Dalia. Directory Assistance strikes again. I'm really sorry. Good-bye," and he slammed the receiver down before she had a chance to answer. The peroxide arrived at the office fifteen minutes later, eyes at half-mast and a face that hadn't been washed yet. "I'm sorry." She yawned. "It took me half an hour to find a cab."

The following morning, when he arrived at the office, there was a woman waiting outside on the sidewalk. She looked about forty, and something about the way she was dressed, about her fragrance, was so not-from-around-here, that when he spoke, he instinctively went for his most genteel pronunciation. Turned out she was looking for a two- or three-room place. She'd prefer to buy, but she didn't rule out a rental, as long as it was available right away. Benny Brokerage said he did happen to have a few nice apartments for sale, and that because the market was in a slump they'd be reasonably priced. He asked her how she'd found him, and she said she'd looked in the Yellow Pages. "Are you Benny?" she asked. He said no—that there hadn't been a Benny for ages, but that he'd kept the name in order not to lose the goodwill. "I'm Michael," he said, smiling. "The truth is that when I'm on the job, even I forget sometimes." "I'm Leah," the woman said, smiling back. "Leah Minster. We spoke on the phone yesterday."

"This is a little uncomfortable," Leah Minster said all of a sudden, out of nowhere. The first apartment had been too dark, and they were walking through the second one. Benny Brokerage tried to play dumb, and started talking about how simple it would be to renovate, and stuff like that, as if she'd been referring to the apartment. "After you phoned me," Leah Minster said, ignoring his reply, "I tried to talk it over with him. At first he lied, but then he got tired of lying, and confessed. That's what the apartment is for. I'm leaving him." Benny Brokerage continued showing her around, thinking to himself that it was none of his business, and that there was no reason for him to get uptight. "Is she young?" Leah Minster persisted, and he nodded and said, "She's not nearly as attractive as you are. I hate having to say a thing like this about a client, but he's an idiot."

The third apartment had better light, and when he showed her the view of the park from the bedroom window, he felt her moving closer, not touching him exactly, but close enough. And even though she liked the apartment, she wanted him to show her another one. In the car, she kept asking him all sorts of questions about the peroxide, and Benny Brokerage tried to put her down but stay kind of vague at the same time. He didn't really feel comfortable, but he went on anyway, because he saw it was making her happy. Whenever they stopped talking, there was a kind of tension, especially at the stoplights, and somehow he just couldn't think of anything to say, the way he usually could, or come up with a little story to take their minds off being stuck. All he could do was stare at the traffic light and wait for it to change. At one of the intersections, even when the light changed, the car in front of them, a Mercedes, didn't move. Benny Brokerage slammed the horn twice and cursed the driver through the window. And when the guy in the Mercedes didn't seem to give a damn, he stormed out of the car. Turned out there was nobody to pick a fight with though, because the driver, who seemed at first to be dozing, didn't wake up, even when Benny Brokerage nudged him. Then the ambulance crew arrived and said it was a stroke. They searched the driver's pockets and the car, but they couldn't find any ID. And Benny Brokerage felt kind of rotten for cursing the guy without a name, and he was sorry for the mean things he'd said about the peroxide too, even though that really had nothing to do with it.

Leah Minster sat beside him in the car, looking pale. He drove her back to the office and made them both some coffee. "The truth is that I didn't tell him anything," she said, and took a sip of the instant. "I was lying actually, just so you'd tell me about her.

I'm sorry, I just had to know." Benny Brokerage smiled and told himself and her that there was no harm done really, that all they'd done was see a couple of apartments and some poor guy who'd dropped dead, and that if there was anything to be learned from the whole experience it was to thank God they were alive— or something along those lines. She finished her coffee, said sorry again, and left. And Michael, who still had a few sips to go, looked around his office, a two-by-three-meter cubicle with a window overlooking the main drag. Suddenly the place seemed so small and transparent, like the ant colony he got for his bar mitzvah a million years ago. And all the goodwill that he'd boasted about so solemnly just two hours earlier sounded like a load of crap. Lately, he didn't much like it when people called him Benny. He didn't like it at all.

PRIDE AND JOY

By the end of the first term, Ehud Guznik was already the tallest boy in his class, maybe even in the whole grade. And besides that, he had a new sports bike, a squat, hairy dog with the eyes of one of those old men who've been waiting in line at the public health clinic all morning, a girlfriend from his class who wouldn't kiss on the mouth but would let him touch the boobs she didn't have, and a straight-A report card, except for geography, and even that was because the teacher was a bitch. In short, Ehud had nothing to complain about, and his parents were bursting with pride. You couldn't bump into them without having to listen to a little anecdote about their amazing child. And people, like people, would nod at them in a mixture of boredom and genuine admiration, and say, "Wonderful, Mr./Mrs. Guznik, that's really wonderful." But what really counts isn't what people say to your face. It's what they say behind your back. And behind their backs, the first thing people said about Max and Felicia Guznik was that they kept getting smaller. Over a single winter, they seemed to have lost at least nine inches each. Mrs. Guznik, once considered imposing, now barely reached the breakfast cereal shelf in the grocery store, and Max too, who once stood close to five-ten, had already moved the car seat all the way forward so he could reach the gas pedal. Very unpleasant, and all the more obvious when they stood next to their giant of a son, only in the fourth grade but already a head taller than his mommy.

Every Tuesday afternoon, Ehud went to the school yard with his father to play basketball. Ehud's father thought Ehud had great potential, because he was both tall and smart. "All through history, the Jews were always considered a smart people, but very short," he liked to explain to Ehud while they practiced shooting baskets. "And every once in a blue moon, when a big schlub did get born, for some reason, he always turned out to be such a knucklehead that you couldn't even teach him what a hook shot is." But you could teach Ehud, and he got better from week to week. And lately, ever since his father started getting shorter, they were evenly matched. "You," his father would tell him on the way home from the court, "you will be a great player some-day, the Moshe Dayan of basketball, except without the patch." The compliments made Ehud very proud, even though he'd never seen Moshe Dayan shoot hoops, but even more than he was proud, he was worried. Worried about the scary way his parents were shrinking. "Maybe all parents are like that," he some-times tried to reassure himself out loud, "and next year, they'll teach us about it in science class." But deep in his heart, he knew something was wrong. Especially after Netta, who'd said yes when he asked her to go steady with him five months before, swore to him on the Bible that her parents, from the time she was little, had stayed more or less the same height. The truth was that he wanted to talk to them about it, but he felt there were things it was better not to talk about. Netta, for example, had a kind of light fuzz on her cheeks, like a beard, and Ehud always pretended he didn't notice, because he thought maybe she herself didn't know and if he told her she'd just feel bad. Maybe it was the same thing with his parents. Or even if they did know, maybe they

were still glad he didn't notice. Things went on like that until after Passover. Ehud's parents kept getting smaller, and he kept act-
ing as if nothing was happening. And the truth is that no one
would ever have figured it out if it hadn't been for Zayde.

From the time he was a puppy, Ehud's dog was attracted to
old people. And that's why his favorite thing was walking in King
David Park, where all the old people from the retirement home
went to get some air. Zayde could sit next to them and listen to
their long stories for hours. They were also the ones who gave
him the name "Zayde"—Grandpa—a name he liked a whole lot
better than the original "Jimmy" he got at the pound. Of all the
old men, Zayde's favorite was an old geezer in a billed cap who
talked to him in Yiddish and fed him blood sausage. Ehud also
liked that old man, who made Ehud swear, the first time they
met, never to get on an elevator with Zayde, because, according
to him, dogs don't understand the concept of an elevator, and going into a kind of small room in one place and then seeing the
doors open on another place altogether shakes their confidence
in their spatial perception and, in general, makes them feel ex-
tremely inadequate. He didn't offer Ehud any blood sausage, but
he did treat him to jelly beans and chocolate coins wrapped in
gold. That old man must have died, or moved to a different home,
because they didn't see him in the park anymore. Sometimes
Zayde still barked and ran after a different old man who looked
enough like him, then whimpered a little when he found out he
was wrong, but that was all.

One day, after Passover, Ehud came home from school in a
bad mood, and when he finished walking Zayde, he didn't feel
like going up the stairs, so they took the elevator. He felt a twinge
as he pressed the 4 button, but said to himself that the old
man was probably dead anyway, which definitely meant he didn't
have to keep his promise. When the elevator door opened, Zayde

peered out, walked back into the elevator, contemplated for a second, and fainted dead away.

Ehud and his frightened parents went straight to the vet, who was quick to reassure them about the dog. But that vet was much more than your ordinary vet. He was a family doctor and a gynecologist from South America who, at some point in his life, for personal reasons, had decided to treat animals. And that doctor needed only one look to realize that the Guzniks were suffering from a rare family disease, a disease that resulted in Ehud's growing taller and taller, but at his parents' expense. "It's simple math," the vet explained. "Every inch added on to the child is an inch subtracted from the parents." "And this disease," Ehud probed, "when does it end?" "End?" The vet tried to camouflage his sorrow behind his thick Argentinean accent. "Only when the parents disappear."

All the way home, Ehud cried and his parents tried to comfort him. Strangely enough, their terrible fate didn't bother them at all. In fact, they almost seemed to enjoy it. "Lots of parents are dying to sacrifice everything for their children," his mother explained to him when he was already in bed, "but not all of them get the chance. Do you know how awful it is to be like Aunt Bella, who sees her son growing up to be short, stupid, and untalented, just like his father, and she can't do a thing about it? Okay, it's true that, in the end, we'll disappear, but so what? In the end, everyone dies, and your father and me, we won't even die, we'll just fade away."

The next day, Ehud went to school without really feeling like it, and got thrown out of Bible class again. He was sitting on the steps near the gym feeling sorry for himself when suddenly he realized something: if every inch he grew was at his parents' expense, all he had to do to save them was stop growing! Ehud hurried to the nurse's office and slyly asked for all the information she had on the subject. From all the brochures she shoved at him, Ehud learned that if he wanted to put up a real fight against growing, what he had to do was smoke a lot, eat very little and at irregular hours, and sleep even less, preferably with lots of interruptions.

He gave his ten-o'clock-recess sandwich to Shiri, a nice, chubby girl from the other fourth-grade class. He ate as little as he could at meals, and to keep people from suspecting, he always passed the meat and dessert to his faithful dog, who waited under the table with sad eyes. The sleeping thing worked out by itself, because since that meeting with the vet, he couldn't sleep for ten minutes without waking up from terrifying, guilt-ridden nightmares. Which left the business with the cigarettes. He smoked two packs a day, cheap and unfiltered. Two whole packs, not one cigarette less. His eyes got red and his mouth filled with a bitter taste, and he also started to cough, an old man's cough, but not for a minute did he think of quitting.

A year and something later, on the day report cards were formally handed out, Matt Zlotnitski and Raz Samara were already taller than he was. Raz also became Netta's new boyfriend after she dumped Ehud on account of the bad breath he'd developed. In fact, that year Ehud's popularity declined. To tell the truth, the kids stopped talking to him completely because they said his chronic cough got on their nerves, and besides, his marks were going down and he wasn't good at sports anymore. The only one who still spoke to him was Shiri, who had started out liking him because of the sandwiches but later took to him because of his personality and other things, and they spent hours together, talking about all kinds of stuff he'd never talked about with Netta. Ehud's parents stopped shrinking at eight inches, and after the doctor confirmed it, Ehud even tried to stop smoking but couldn't. He went to an acupuncturist and a hypnotist, and they both said that the main reason he couldn't stop was pampering and character, but Shiri, who actually liked the smell of the cigarettes, consoled him by saying that it really didn't matter.

On Saturdays, Ehud would put his parents in his shirt pocket and take them for a bike ride. He pedaled slowly enough for the stout Zayde to keep up with them, and when his parents fought inside his pocket, or just got tired of each other, he would move one of them to another pocket. Once, Shiri even went with them, and they rode to the park and had a real picnic. And on the way back, when they stopped to look at the sunset, Ehud's father whispered loudly to him from his pocket, "Kiss her. Kiss her!" which was a little embarrassing. Ehud quickly changed the subject and talked to her about the sun and how hot and big it was and all kinds of things like that, until it was dark, and his parents fell asleep deep in his pocket. When he'd exhausted all his stories about the sun and they'd almost reached Shiri's house, he told her about the moon and the stars too, and their effect on each other, and when those stories were finished too, he coughed and shut up. And Shiri said to him, "Kiss me," and he kissed her. "Way to go, son!" he could hear his father whisper from the depths of his pocket, and he felt his emotional mother jab him with her elbow and softly weep with joy.

SURPRISE EGG

To Danny, with love

Listen, a true story. About three months ago a woman about thirty-two years old met her death in a suicide bomb attack near a bus stop. She wasn't the only one who met her death, lots of others did too. But this story is about her.

People who are killed in terrorist attacks are taken to the Forensic Institute in Abu Kabir for an autopsy. Many people in important positions in Israeli society have wondered about this procedure, and even the people who work at Abu Kabir don't always understand it exactly. The cause of death in those attacks is known, after all, and a body isn't some surprise egg that you open without knowing what you're going to find inside—a sailboat maybe, or a race car, or a toy koala. I mean, whenever they operate they always find the same things—little pieces of metal, nails, or other kinds of shrapnel. Very few surprises, in other words. But in this case, of the thirty-two-year-old woman, they did find something else. Inside her body, besides all those pieces of metal that had torn into her flesh, this woman had dozens of tumors, really big ones. There were tumors in her stomach, in her liver, and in her intestines, but especially in her head. When the pathologist peeked into her skull, the first thing he said was "Oh my God" because it was simply frightening. He saw dozens of tumors that had inched their way into her brain like a swarm of cruel ants that just wanted to devour more and more.

And this is where the scientific observation comes in: if this woman hadn't died in a terrorist attack, she would have collapsed within a week and would have died from her tumors within a month, two months tops. It's hard to see how a young woman like that could have suffered from such an advanced cancer without its being diagnosed at all. Maybe she was one of those people who don't like medical examinations or maybe she figured the pain and the dizziness she'd been suffering from were something routine that would just go away. In any case, when her husband arrived to identify her at the morgue, the pathologist had a hard time deciding whether to tell him about it or not. On the one hand, it was a revelation that could have offered some comfort— there's no point in tormenting yourself with thoughts like "if only she hadn't gone to work that day" or "if only I'd driven her" when you know that your wife was about to die no matter what. On the other hand, this news could make the grief even more distressing and turn her arbitrary and horrible death into something much more horrible: a death experienced twice over in a sense, making it inevitable, as if someone up there wanted to make absolutely sure, and no what-ifs could have saved her, not even hypothetically. Then again, the pathologist thought, what difference did it really make? The woman was dead, her husband was a widower, her children were orphans—that's what mattered, that's what was sad, and all the rest was neither here nor there.

The husband asked to identify his wife by her foot. Most people identify their loved ones by their faces. But he asked to identify her by her foot, because he thought that if he saw her dead face, the sight would haunt him his whole life, or rather, what remained of it. He had loved her and he knew her so well that he could identify her by each and every part of her body, and somehow her foot seemed the most remote, neutral, far-removed. He looked at the foot for another few seconds, even after he'd identified the barely visible wavy contours of her toenails, the slightly crooked, chubby big toe, the perfect arching of her sole. Maybe it was a bad idea, he thought to himself as he continued to look at the little foot (size 5), maybe it was a bad idea to choose the foot. A dead person's face looks like a sleeping person's, but with a dead person's foot there was no mistaking the death under every toenail. "That's her," he told the pathologist after a while, and left the room.

Among the people at the woman's funeral was the pathologist. He wasn't the only one. There was the mayor of Jerusalem, and the minister of internal security. Both of them made personal promises to the husband, repeating his name and the deceased woman's name many times as they spoke, to avenge her brutal death. They gave a dramatic and vivid description of how they would hunt down those responsible for dispatching the murderer (there was no way of taking revenge on the suicide bomber himself). The husband looked rather uneasy with the promises they made. It seemed that he wasn't all that interested, and the only reason he was trying to hide it was to avoid hurting the feelings of the impassioned public figures who were naïve enough to believe that their vehement speeches could offer him some solace.

The funeral was the second time the pathologist had considered the idea of telling the husband that his wife had been on the verge of death in any case, to offset some of the uneasiness and vengefulness in the air, but this time too he kept it to himself. On his way home he tried to think philosophically about everything that had happened. What is cancer, he thought to himself, if not an attack of terror from above? What is it that God is doing if not terrorizing us in protest against . . . something. Something so lofty and transcendental that it lies beyond our grasp? Like his work at the institute, this thought too was surgically precise, but it didn't really make any difference.

The night after the funeral, the husband had a sad dream in which the dead foot was rubbing against his face, a dream that caused him to wake up in a state of fright and agitation. He tip-toed into the kitchen, so as not to wake the children, and made himself a cup of tea without turning on the light. Even after he'd finished drinking the steaming tea, he went on sitting in the dark kitchen. He tried to think of something he'd like to do, some-thing that would make him happy, anything. Even something he couldn't really allow himself because of the kids or because he couldn't afford to, but nothing like that came to mind. He felt as though he was stuffed full of some dense and sour material that was blocking his chest, and it wasn't grief. It was something much more serious than grief. After all those years, life now seemed like no more than a trap, a maze—not even a maze, just a room that was all walls, with no door. There must be something, he persisted, something I want, even if I can't make it happen. Anything.

Some people commit suicide after someone close to them goes, others turn to religion, and there are some who sit in the kitchen all night and don't even wait for the sun to rise. The light from outside was beginning to creep into the apartment and pretty soon the little ones would be waking up. He tried to recall once more the feel of the foot in the dream and, the way it always happens with dreams, all he could do was reconstruct it but not really experience it. "If only she hadn't gone to work that day," he thought, forcing himself to get up. "If only I'd driven her. She'd still be alive now, sitting here in the kitchen with me."

DIRT

So let's say I'm dead now, or I open a self-service laundromat, the first one in Israel. I rent a small place, a little rundown, on the south side, and paint everything blue. At first, there are only four machines and a special dispenser that sells tokens. Then I put in a TV and even a pinball machine. Or else I'm on my bathroom floor with a bullet in my head. My father finds me. At first, he doesn't notice the blood. He thinks I'm dozing or playing one of my stupid games. It's only when he touches the back of my neck and feels something hot and sticky oozing from his fingers toward his arm that he realizes something's wrong. People who come to do their washing in a self-service laundromat are lonely people. You don't have to be a genius to figure that out. And me, I'm really no genius, and I did. That's why I always try to create an atmosphere in the laundromat that will make people feel less lonely. Lots of TVs. Dispensers that say thank you in a human voice for buying the tokens, pictures of mass rallies on the walls. The tables for folding laundry are set up so that lots of people have to use them at the same time. Not because I'm stingy; it's on purpose. Lots of couples met at my place because of those tables. People who used to be lonely and now they have someone, maybe more than one, who lies next to them at night, shoves them in their sleep. The first thing my father does is wash his hands. Only then does he call for an ambulance. That hand washing is going to cost him dearly. He won't forgive himself till his dying day. He'll even be ashamed to tell people. How his son is lying there next to him, dying, and him, instead of feeling grief or compassion or fear, something, all he can feel is revulsion. That laundromat will turn into a chain. A chain that'll be big, especially in Tel Aviv, but it'll do well in the suburbs too. The logic behind its success will be simple—wherever there are lonely people and dirty laundry, they'll always come to me. After my mother dies, even my father will come into one of those branches to do his laundry. He'll never meet a woman or make a friend there, but the chance that he might will drive him there every single time, will give him a tiny sliver of hope.

ACTUALLY, I'VE HAD SOME PHENOMENAL HARD-ONS LATELY

When Ronel woke up that magical Tuesday morning and found his beloved terrier, Darko, between his legs licking his morning erection, a single razor-sharp thought passed through his dull and relatively unoccupied brain: "Is this sexual?" In other words, was Darko licking his balls the same way he licked Schneider's balls—Schneider being the miniature schnauzer Darko tried to have sexual intercourse with every time they bumped into each other in Meir Park—or was Darko licking his master's penis for the same reason he licked the dewdrops off a fragrant leaf in that park? It was a troubling question, though not as troubling as the question of whether Neeva, his wide-hipped wife, suspected him of sleeping with his business partner, Renana, which would explain why she was so nasty to her on the phone, or was that sheer dislike? "Oh, Darko, Darko," Ronel muttered to himself with a mixture of self-pity and affection, "you're the only one who really loves me." Darko, who might not have recognized a human male sex organ as such, recognized his name every time, and he responded with a bark of joy. Clearly, it was better to be a dog coping with dog-dilemmas, like the what-tree-should-I-pee-on-this-morning one, than to be Ronel grappling with such tedious moral quandaries as whether fucking Renana as she bent over his wife's vanity table was less repellent than fucking her right in their queen-size bed. A question that had many implications, by the way. Because if it didn't matter, they'd be a lot more comfortable doing it on the bed, and that would be that. Or, for example, whether fantasizing about his naked wife while penetrating Renana offset the infidelity somewhat, or whether it was just another perversion? "Daddy's not a pervert, Darko honey," Ronel said as he stretched and got out of bed. "Daddy's a complex person." "What?" Neeva asked, peering into the bedroom. "Did you say something?" "I told Darko I'd be home late because I have a meeting with the Germans tonight," Ronel said, making the most of the rare eye contact with his wife. "Oh, really?" Neeva sneered. "And what did Darko have to say about that?" "Nothing," Ronel said, putting on a pair of gray underpants. "Darko accepts me." "Darko also accepts Purina Dog Chow," Neeva snapped. "His standards aren't exactly high."

One obvious advantage of having an affair with a colleague was that all those romantic candlelight dinners were tax deductible. It wasn't the only bonus, of course, but it was undoubtedly the one Ronel enjoyed most, because he never felt more relaxed and at peace than when he was stapling receipts to pieces of paper embellished with details and dates in his own handwriting. And when the invoice wasn't just his ticket to a tax deduction but an emotionally charged object in its own right, one that allowed him to reminisce about a night of successful lovemaking, the pleasure it gave was doubled. "I need a receipt for my taxes," he said to the waiter, stressing the word "taxes," as if there were more than one kind of receipt in this little world of ours. The

waiter nodded at Ronel as if to say he knew the score. Ronel
didn't like him. Maybe because of the niggling way he corrected
their pronunciation when they ordered, maybe because he'd insisted on hiding his left arm behind his back throughout the meal,
which made Ronel nervous. Or maybe it was just because he was
a waiter who earned his living from tips, a form of payment that
irritated Ronel because it had no place in the cozy womb of deductible expenses.

"What's with you tonight?" Renana asked after they'd decided to abandon a failed attempt at wild sex in favor of watching
the E Channel together and eating watermelon. "I'm stressed,"
Ronel said, "stressed and a little weak, physically." "You were
stressed last time too. And on Thursday, we didn't even try. Tell
me . . ." She stopped speaking in order to swallow an especially
large piece of watermelon, and as he waited out the lengthy
process of her swallowing, Ronel knew he was in for a hassle.
And in fact, a belch later, Renana picked up right where she'd left
off. ". . . do you still fuck your wife or can't you do it with her either?" "What do you mean, 'either'?" Ronel said. Now he was annoyed. "What, to be more precise, do you mean 'can't do it with
her either'? Is there something we don't do?" "Fuck," Renana
said, licking her stubby fingers. "We don't fuck. Not that it's a big
deal or anything. It's just that, when you're 'a fuck on the side'
and the whole sex thing drops out of the equation, then you're
nothing but 'on the side,' if you know what I mean. I'm not saying it's a deal breaker or anything, it's just, you know, a little
weird. Because with your wife, even if you don't fuck, you can
visit her parents or fight about who loads the dishwasher, all the
normal couple things. But when it happens with a lover, it sort of
pulls the rug out." "Who said we don't fuck?" "Your prick," Renana said without a hint of provocation in her voice. "That's why
I asked about your wife, you know, to see if it's because I don't

turn you on anymore. Or if it's something more . . ." "More what?" Ronel insisted as the pause lengthened. "Give me a sec," Renana mumbled, "I'm looking for a gentler word than 'impotent.'" "You're making a big deal over nothing," Ronel said, getting angry. "Just because once or twice I was a little bit tired and stressed out over work, it doesn't mean I'm impotent. I had a hard-on just this morning. Not an ordinary hard-on, either. It was phenomenal." Ronel, remembering Darko, felt his organ stiffen a little and, for no reason, was flooded with guilt. "Terrific," Renana said. "That's good news. And who got to share this phenomenal hard-on of yours, Neeva?" "No," Ronel said, momentarily confused. "I shared it with myself." "How nice for you." Renana smiled her famous carrion-eating smile, which he'd previously come across only at work, and went back to licking the watermelon juice off the palm of her hand.

Even so, the night might have ended with a fuck. Not a passionate fuck, but an angry one, with Ronel trying to work up some desire and have an erection, if only to make Renana eat her words. Maybe. Who knows. But Ronel's cell phone vibrated in his shirt pocket right where his heart should have been and brought that utterly pathetic evening to a new low. "Sorry to disturb you in the middle of your meeting with the Germans." He heard Neeva's hate-filled voice stretching out the word "Germans" as if she were referring to Hitler himself. "Don't be silly, sweetheart, you're not disturbing me at all. We just finished," Ronel said, sucking up to Neeva the way he always did around clients. To sound more credible, he even tossed a few words in English at Renana: "It's my wife. She says hello." Renana promptly gave a loud belch in reply. "Mr. Mattenklott says hello, too," Ronel said, afraid Neeva might have heard the repulsive belch, and added quickly, "I think he's had one too many. I'll just drop him and Ingo at the hotel and come home." "Ronel," Neeva rebuked him on the other end of the line, "I didn't call to find out when you're coming home. I called to tell you something." "I know, I know. I'm sorry," Ronel apologized automatically as he tried to grab the remote from Renana, who was raising the volume. "It's your dog," Neeva added after a short silence. "He ran away."

When a dog takes a thin little saw and saws through the bars on the bathroom window, then shimmies down some tied-together sheets, you can say, "The dog ran away." But when you're walking down the street with him and he's not on a leash, and an hour later you realize he's nowhere to be seen, then someone has clearly fucked up. Trying to lay the blame on Darko wasn't fair. "He was probably sniffing some curb or monument and when he looked up, he realized you weren't there," he said to Neeva in an accusing tone as they walked down King George Street trying to reconstruct the route of that disastrous evening stroll. "How many times have I told you not to let him out of your sight?" "Tell me," Neeva said as she stopped walking and stood in the middle of the street like a wife about to make a scene. "What exactly are you trying to say? That I'm not a good enough au pair for your smelly dog? That I don't walk him according to the rules of the International Dog-Walkers' Association? If you were home instead of fucking around with your *Germans*, you could've taken him out yourself and none of this would've happened." Ronel could have complained about how he worked his ass off till all hours just to put food on the table, but he decided, for tactical reasons, to hold his peace. One of the first things he'd learned in the business world was never to reach a point of no return. You always left open as many options as possible. This often meant not saying or doing the thing you wanted to say or do. Now, for example, he felt very much like kicking Neeva in the shin as hard as he could. Not only because she'd let Darko run away, but also because she didn't call him by his name and insisted on referring to him as "smelly," and mainly because she refused to take responsibility for her actions and behaved as if this terrible tragedy were God's way of punishing Ronel and not the mistake of a self-centered and totally irresponsible wife. He didn't kick her in the shin as hard as he could because that, as mentioned, would have been a point of no return. Instead, with that same composure and self-control so often displayed by murderers when cleaning up the scene of the crime and getting rid of their victims' bodies, Ronel suggested that she go home and wait there in case someone called with information about Darko. "Who's going to call?" Neeva laughed. "Your stupid dog from a pay phone? Or his kidnappers asking for ransom? Even if someone does find him, they won't know our number." "I still think it would be better if we split up," Ronel insisted, and seriously considered abandoning the insight that had served him so well for so many years and kicking Neeva very hard after all. When she persisted in asking why, he shook his head wildly and said, "No reason."

Ronel leaned against a yellow mailbox and read over the list he'd just made on the back of the receipt from the restaurant he and Renana had eaten in that night. The list was headed "Places Darko Likes (?)" He didn't know why he'd tacked on that question mark and parentheses. Maybe because he felt that if the list didn't include an element of uncertainty, it would be like claiming he knew all there was to know about Darko, whereas Ronel himself had readily admitted countless times, to himself and to others, that he didn't always understand Darko. Why sometimes he barked and other times chose not to. Why he started digging holes so furiously, then left the excavation as suddenly as he'd started it, for no obvious reason. Did he think of Ronel as his master? His father? His friend? Maybe even as his lover? At any rate, it was definitely no more than a list to help Ronel search, and that's why it needed a question mark of uncertainty. The first place on the list was Meir Park, where he and Darko went every morning. That was where Darko met the dogs who were his friends and enemies, not to mention his bosom buddy, the stumpy Schneider. At that late hour, there were no dogs or people in Meir Park. Only a drunk, homeless Russian dozing on a bench. Ronel presumed he was Russian not just because of the somewhat stereotypical bottle of vodka cradled in his arms, but because he kept laughing and speaking Russian in his sleep. Ronel stopped for a minute and said to himself that despite the troubles that kept plaguing him and sometimes made him feel like a latter-day Job, or at least a Job lite, he should be grateful for what he had and thank whoever it is nonreligious people thank about such things for not putting him in that Russian guy's torn old newspaper-stuffed shoes. The Russian's laughter grew deeper and louder, demolishing Ronel's ideas about his own relative happiness. "Who says?" Ronel asked, suddenly filled with a great truth diluted by a substantial amount of self-pity. "Who says my fate is better than his? Here I am in the same park where he's drunk and happy. And I'm neither drunk nor happy. All I have in the world is a dog who left me, a wife I don't really love, and a business . . ." It was actually the thought of his business that cheered him up a little. This was, after all, a period of some growth, which hardly held out a promise of boundless joy but, for now, was still preferable to newspaper in his shoes.

Near the park exit, Ronel noticed a rapid dog-like movement in the bushes. But after observing it briefly, he saw that the object of his shattered hope was the short, bearded shadow of Schneider. Ronel, who frequented the park only during the day, was surprised to see Schneider there so late at night. His first thought was that some sixth sense had told Schneider that Darko was lost and he'd left his house to join the search, but a familiar whistle punctured that heroic interpretation of events. And right after the whistle came Alma, Schneider's beautiful, limping mistress. Alma, who was about twenty-five, was one of the most beautiful women Ronel knew, and definitely the lamest. She'd been injured in an unusually stupid car accident, and had used the money she received in settlement to buy a fully renovated penthouse on Michal Street. Alma's extreme encounter with a bad driver and an excellent lawyer (she'd even told Ronel his name once, but since there were no injury suits on his horizon, he quickly forgot it) had undoubtedly shifted the course of her life. People always say they would pass up any amount of money to get their health back, but was that really true? Alma, as far as he could tell from a leash away, always smiled a genuine-looking smile, which Ronel had tried to imitate for business purposes. He had even practiced a few times in front of the mirror before he gave up and opted for one that came more naturally. Hers was a permanent smile that rested on her face, a default smile, not fixed or phony, but always in reaction to whatever was happening around it—broadening, narrowing, turning surprised or cynical when called for, but always there and always relaxed. It was the relaxation of that smile that made Ronel try to mimic it, recognizing its superiority as a negotiating tool over any other expression. Would she have smiled that way if she were poor and had a platinum-free leg? Or would the smile have been different, less serene? More frightened by an uncertain economic future, by the threat of old age looming over her perfect beauty?

"I didn't know you and Darko came here at night," Alma said, hopping into the shaft of light at the entrance to the park. "We don't," Ronel groaned desperately. "Darko ran away," he said, but quickly corrected himself. "I mean he got lost." Schneider was looking all around Ronel with the annoying friskiness of a stupid and not particularly sensitive schnauzer. "He doesn't understand," Alma apologized. "He smells Darko on your clothes and thinks he's here." "I know, I know," Ronel said, nodding, and for no reason, burst into tears. "But he's not. He's not here. He could be dead by now. Run over. Or maybe some kids are torturing him in a backyard, putting out cigarettes on him, or maybe the city dogcatchers got him . . ." Alma put a comforting hand on his arm, and even though her hand was damp with sweat, there was something pleasant about that dampness, something gentle and alive. "Dogcatchers don't work at night, and Darko's a smart dog. There's no way he was run over. If it were Schneider . . ." she said, giving her lively schnauzer the kind of sad, loving look beautiful girls always save for their ugly girlfriends, "then we'd have to worry. But Darko knows how to take care of himself. I can just see him whining outside the entrance to your building. Or on your doormat right now, chewing on a stolen bone."

Even though he could have called Neeva to ask whether Darko had come back, Ronel decided to go home. It was close by, and besides, now that Alma had managed to convince him that Darko might be there, he didn't want Neeva to be the one to tell him the good news. "She and I," he thought, "should have separated a long time ago." Once, he remembered, he'd looked at Neeva when she was sleeping and imagined a horrible scenario in which she died in a terrorist attack. He'd be sorry for cheating on her and he'd cry live on the six o'clock news out of guilt cunningly disguised as pure grief. That thought, he now remembered, had been sad and terrible, but, to his surprise, it also made him feel a kind of relief. As if her being wiped out of his life might open up a space for something else, something with color and smell and life. But before he could feel guilty again about this sensation of relief, Renana made her entrance into the scenario and now that Neeva was no longer in the picture, she moved right in with him, at first to give him comfort and support. Then she stayed for no reason at all. Ronel remembered how he'd gone on and on in his imagination, till he reached the point when Renana said to him, "It's me or Darko." He chose Darko and remained alone in his apartment. Without a woman. Without love, except for Darko's, whose existence only intensified the terrible loneliness he called his life. "Terrorism is awful," Ronel had thought that night. "It destroys life in an instant," and he gave Neeva's sleeping forehead a gentle kiss.

Ronel walked past Darko almost without noticing him. He was too busy trying to find a lighted window in his third-floor apartment. Darko was busy too, his filmy glance admiringly following the quick hands of the owner of Tarboosh Shwarma as they cut thin slices of meat from the revolving spit. But when the two friends finally spotted each other, their reunion was replete with lavish face-licking and emotion. "That's some dog," the shwarma guy said as he knelt in front of Darko, placing a piece of paper with a few greasy slices of meat on the sidewalk like a high priest making a sacrifice to his god. "I want you to know that a lot of dogs come here, and I don't give them anything. But this one . . ." he said, pointing at Darko. "Tell me, does he happen to be Turkish?" "What do you mean, Turkish?" Ronel asked, offended. "Oh nothing," the shwarma guy apologized. "I'm from Izmir, so I thought . . . When I was a kid, I had a dog just like him, a puppy. But he used to pee in the house, which drove my mother crazy, so she threw him out, like he did it on purpose. But you, you're a good man. He ran away from you and you're not even mad. Believe me, that's how it should be. I don't understand all those tough guys who clobber their dogs with the leash if they stop for a minute to watch the shwarma turn. What are they, Nazis?" "He didn't run away," Ronel corrected him as he pressed his tired forehead against Darko's sturdy back. "He got lost."

That night, Ronel decided to write a book. Something between an educational fable and a philosophical treatise. The story

would be about a king beloved by all his subjects who loses something he cherishes, not money, maybe a child or something, or a
nightingale, if nobody's used that yet. Around page one hundred,
the book would turn into something less symbolic and more
modern that dealt with man's alienation in contemporary society
and offered a little consolation. On about page one hundred sixty
or seventy, it would change into a kind of airplane novel in terms
of readability, but of much higher quality. And on page three
hundred, the book would turn into a furry little animal readers
could hug and pet, as a way of coping with their loneliness. He
hadn't yet decided on what sort of technology would turn the
book into that ever-so-touchable animal, but he pointed out to
himself before he fell asleep that in the last few years, both mo-
lecular biology and publishing had taken giant steps forward and
were crying out now to join forces.

And that same night, Ronel had a dream, and in his dream he
was sitting on the balcony of his house concentrating on the
newspaper in a courageous and sincere effort to solve the enigma
of human existence. His beloved dog, Darko, suddenly appeared
on the balcony wearing a gray suit, a giant bone in his mouth. He
put the bone down at his feet and hinted to Ronel with a tilt of his
head that he should look for the answer in the financial pages.
Then he explained in a deep, human voice, which sounded a little like his father's voice, that the human race is nothing but a tax
dodge. "A tax dodge?" Ronel repeated, confused. "Yes," Darko
said, nodding his clever head. He explained to Ronel that his tax
consultant, an extraterrestrial who lived on the planet Darko
originally came from, had advised him to invest his earnings in an
ecologically oriented enterprise, because ecology was big with the
extraterrestrial IRS. And that, using shell corporations, he soon
got involved in the whole field of developing life and species on
planets. "In general," Darko explained, "everyone knows there's

no real money in developing the human race. Or any other race, for that matter. But since it's a new field that's wide open taxationally, there's nothing to stop me from submitting a mountain of receipts." "I don't believe it," Ronel said in his dream. "I refuse to believe that our only function in this world is to be a tax shelter so my beloved dog can launder money." "First of all," Darko corrected him, "no one's talking about money laundering here. All my revenue's clean and aboveboard, I don't go in for anything shady. All we're talking about here is a semilegitimate inflation of expenses. And secondly, let's say I grant your first premise that it isn't humanity's real function to be a tax shelter for me, OK? If we take this argument a little further, what other function could it have? I'm not asking pragmatically, but theoretically." Darko kept quiet for a little while, and when he saw Ronel didn't have a single answer in his arsenal, he barked twice, picked up the bone with his mouth and left the balcony. "Don't go," Ronel begged in a whisper. "Please, don't leave me, my dog, my friend, my love . . ."

That morning too, Ronel woke up with a glorious hard-on and Darko's as-yet-to-be-defined licking. When he finally opened his eyes, Darko was running around the room boneless and completely naked. "It's not sexual," was the first thought that came into Ronel's mind. "It's sociable, maybe even existential." "Darko, my angel, my friend," he whispered, trying to contain the overwhelming joy he felt so as not to wake Neeva, "you're the only one who really loves me."

MORE LIFE

This is one story you've got to hear! Two identical twin brothers from Jacksonville, Florida, met two identical twin sisters from Daytona Beach. They met through the Internet. Or to be exact, it started with just one couple, Nicky and Todd, and when Todd brought Nicky home for dinner at his parents' place, his twin brother, Adam, got really excited. That's when Todd told him she had a sister. Not just a sister, an identical twin. Todd and Nicky set up this blind date. Of course it couldn't exactly be called a blind date, considering that Adam and Michelle both knew what the other person would look like. To make things less awkward, they turned it into a double date and the four of them went to see a movie at the drive-in. And what movie did they go see? No, not *Twins* with Schwarzenegger and DeVito. They went to see *Les Liaisons dangereuses*. Can you imagine? There couldn't be a worse movie for a blind date—it's all intrigues and cheating and lies—and yet it went well. After the movie they drove to a diner. The girls made a point of dressing in different colors so it would be easier to tell them apart. The guys came in jeans and white T-shirts, looking exactly the same. And at one embarrassing point that she'd still remember years later, Nicky made the mistake of kissing Adam, because she thought he was Todd.

When you meet someone and fall in love, what's the strongest emotion you have? I don't know about you, but what I always feel when that happens is that I'm with someone who's completely unlike anyone else in the world. But when Michelle and Adam were sitting across from each other in the diner, what did they tell themselves? That there was no other man in the world like Adam? That there was nobody else at the table like Michelle? Whatever they might have thought at that moment, in the end it led to marriage. Well, actually I'm wrong—in the end it led to death. But at some stage in between, it led to marriage.

When Michelle and Adam got married, it was a year after Todd had slipped the ring on Nicky's finger. Identical twin sisters married to identical twin brothers. I don't know if there's ever been anything like it in all of history. Forget the history of Florida, the history of the world. It was so uncanny, they were even approached by a talk show, and I don't mean some local affiliate. Someone from NBC, but Michelle said no, because she claimed that if she went on the show she'd feel like a bearded lady. "I mean, it's not like they're asking us because of anything we did. The only reason they want us on the show is because they think it's weird. I bet they'll tell us to dress the same and they'll start asking Nicky and me why we've got the same haircut, and even if we try to explain it's because that's the haircut that looks best on us, it'll still come out perverted," she told Adam with great conviction. "They want us there like some freak show. And I bet the host will make fun of us and tell lots of little jokes and make us look bad. And the audience at home will laugh, and you and Todd will laugh, because you and Todd laugh at everything, and I'll be the only one who's dying of embarrassment." The truth was, Adam would have loved to be on the show. He'd never been on

TV, and he knew how impressed the guys at work would be if they saw him on a talk show, and so would the customers. He'd have enjoyed the hell out of it, but he didn't even try to reason with her. Because once Michelle had made up her mind, there was no point, she'd never listen to a word that anybody said. In the end, Adam did wind up on TV—prime time no less, coast-to-coast. It wasn't exactly in the studio, but they showed him for al-most one whole minute in a home video his dad had taken years before, playing basketball with Todd. It was a segment where he was waving at the camera, and Todd took advantage of it to grab the ball away from him and shoot a basket. "Even then," the an-nouncer in the studio intoned, "you could sense the rivalry be-tween them." And it wasn't as if there *had* ever been any rivalry, but that's how it is on TV. They love to blow things out of propor-tion, for dramatic effect. And if they can't find anything to blow up out of proportion, they make it up.

In real life, Adam and Todd had actually been on very good terms. Altogether the two couples got along great. They lived near each other, and spent their weekends with one another. And when they started talking about having a family, they even fig-ured on having kids at more or less the same time, so they'd grow up together. And those plans would probably have worked out, if it wasn't for what happened. And it's not that anyone suspected anything. Even looking back, it was hard to suspect such a thing. And even if one of the neighbors did happen to see Adam and Nicky kissing on the street or on the porch, they probably took Adam for Todd, or figured that she must be Michelle.

And their affair went on that way for more than a year. At one point, they even thought of coming out with it, telling the whole world, getting divorced and marrying each other. But Nicky knew it would destroy Michelle, and Adam felt a little sorry for her too, and also for Todd, because even if Todd had hurt him once in the past, maybe more than once, he'd always loved Adam and only wanted what was best for him. Then there was a point when Nicky suggested that they stop. That was when she'd begun to think that Todd might be catching on. Nothing definite, she just had a feeling, and they really did stop seeing each other for a few weeks, but then they got back together, because the separation turned out to be more than either of them could bear.

I only met Nicky a few years after the whole business ended badly. Adam was dead by then, and Todd had already done a lot of time for it. Michelle hadn't spoken a word to her since the whole thing came out, which in her case was on the day Todd put three bullets in Adam's head at point-blank range. Michelle had never exactly been the forgiving type. I had arrived as a guest lecturer at the university and Nicky was the department secretary. I first heard her story from another teacher on the faculty, a guest too, from Turkey, and then from her. She and I wound up getting pretty close that year, and at some stage she told me what had happened. Even before we slept together.

She said she'd left Florida to get away from it all, but that it hadn't really made a difference because everyone here knew about it too, and they all talked about it behind her back. She said that in some strange way, "perverse" is what her sister Michelle would probably have called it, she really missed the whole twin-hood thing, the way people they'd meet would confuse her with Michelle. "Somehow," I remember her telling me, just before we kissed for the first time, "when you've got an identical twin sister in the same neighborhood, you feel more. As if you're more than one person and you've got more than one life to live. The very fact that someone tells you 'I saw you an hour ago eating vanilla ice cream' or 'I saw you at the bus stop in a pink dress'—you can explain it was your sister if you want, but somehow you feel like it really was you having that ice cream or wearing that pink dress.

It's a strange feeling, like you're living another life and using your expanded life to do all these mysterious things you'll never really know." That's not all she missed, she missed her husband too, and above all she missed Adam, a guy who was the spitting image— but the absolute spitting image—of her jailed husband, and someone she loved a lot more, even if she couldn't say why.

That night I told her about my own life too, and about my affair. Not with my wife's sister. Just a girl at work who didn't look anything like my wife. She was younger than my wife and much less attractive, but I felt then the same way Nicky did, that I was getting myself more life. Not necessarily a better life, not a life more promising than the one I already had. But because I thought this life was in addition to and not instead of, I devoured it without a second's hesitation. In my case, nobody shot anybody and even though my wife suspected something, I never got caught. She and I stayed together. Except that, like everything in life that seems to come for free, that affair at work cost something too. When they offered me this job abroad for a year she preferred to stay home. The official reason was the kids, that the move would be hard on them, but the truth was that maybe it suited both of us to be apart for a while. When I met Nicky it was long after I'd promised myself I'd never cheat on my wife again. But I did anyway, and it wasn't any great love story, nothing like that, just a chance to gain that much more life.

GLITTERY EYES

This is a story about a little girl who loved glittery things more than anything else in the whole world. She had a glittery dress, and glittery socks, and glittery ballet slippers. And a glittery black doll named Christie after their maid. Even her teeth glittered, though her father insisted that they sparkled, which wasn't quite the same. "Glittery," she thought to herself, "is the color of fairy godmothers, and that's why it's the prettiest color of all." On Make-Believe Day in kindergarten, she dressed up as a fairy godmother, and sprinkled glitter over everyone who came near her, and said it was wishing powder. If you mixed it with water, it would make your wish come true, and if they went home right away and mixed it with water, then it would work for them too. It was a very real-looking costume, and it won her first prize in the costume competition. And the teacher, Lily, said that if she hadn't known her from before, if she just saw her by chance on the street, she would be sure the little girl was a real fairy godmother.

When the little girl got home, she took off her costume, stood there in nothing but her underpants, threw all of her glitter up into the air, and shouted: "I want glittery eyes!" She shouted it so loud that her mother came running to see if everything was all right. "I want glittery eyes," the little girl said, quietly this time, and kept on saying it the whole time she was in the shower, but even after that, when her mother dried her off and helped her into her pajamas, her eyes remained the ordinary kind. Very very green, and very very pretty, but no glitter. "With glittery eyes, I'd be able to do so many things," she said, trying to persuade her mother, who seemed to be losing her patience. "I'd be able to walk along the street at night, and the drivers would see me from far away, and when I got older, I'd be able to read in the dark and save a lot on electricity, and whenever you lost me at the movies you'd always be able to find me right away, without calling the usher." "What's all this nonsense about glittery eyes?" her mother said, and pulled out a cigarette. "There's no such thing anyway. Who put that ridiculous idea in your head?" "Yes, there is!" the little girl shouted, and jumped up and down on her bed. "There is, there is, there is, and besides, you're not supposed to smoke around me. It's bad for my health." "OK," her mother said, "OK. Look, it isn't even lit." And she put the cigarette back. "Now get into bed like a good girl, and tell me who's been talking to you about glittery eyes. Don't tell me it's that fat teacher of yours?" "She isn't fat," the little girl said, "and it wasn't her. Nobody talked to me about it. I saw it for myself. There's this dirty little boy in our kindergarten class and he has them." "And what's the dirty little boy's name?" The little girl shrugged. "I don't know. He's kind of dirty and he always keeps quiet and sits far away from everyone. But I'm telling you, his eyes glitter. And I want eyes like that too." "So go over to him tomorrow and ask him where he got them," her mother suggested, "and when he tells you, we'll go there, and get them for you too." "And until tomorrow?" the little girl asked. "Until tomorrow, go to sleep," her mother said. "I'm going outside for a smoke."

The next day, the little girl made her father take her to kindergarten very very early, because she just couldn't wait, and she wanted to ask the dirty little boy where to get glittery eyes. But it didn't do her any good, because the dirty little boy arrived last, long after everyone else. And today he wasn't even dirty. His clothes were still a little old, and they had stains on them, but he himself looked as if he'd had a bath and someone seemed to have run a comb through his hair. "Tell me," she said, turning to him without a second's hesitation, "where do you get such glittery eyes?" "It's not on purpose," the almost-combed little boy apologized. "It just happens." "And what do I have to do for it to just happen to me too?" the little girl cried out. "I think you need to want something an awful lot, and when it still doesn't happen, your eyes start to glitter, just like that." "That's stupid," the girl said, getting angry. "Look, I want glittery eyes an awful lot, and it doesn't happen, so why don't they glitter like yours?" "I don't know," the boy said, scared because she was angry. "I only know about myself, not about other people." "I'm sorry I yelled," she reassured him, touching him with her tiny hand. "Maybe you only have to want certain kinds of things. Tell me, what did you want so badly, and you didn't get?" "A girl," the boy stammered. "To be my girlfriend." "Is that all?" the little girl exclaimed. "But that's easy. Tell me who she is, and I'll make her become your girlfriend. And if she won't, I'll make sure nobody talks to her anymore." "I can't," the little boy said. "I'm too shy." "All right," the little girl said. "It doesn't really matter. And it wouldn't solve my problem anyway, or get me glittery eyes. Besides, that could never happen to me. If I ever wanted someone to be my girlfriend, they'd want to, because they all want to be my girlfriend." "You," the little boy blurted out. "I want you to be my girlfriend."

For a few seconds, the little girl didn't say anything, because the dirty little boy had taken her by surprise. Then she touched him again with her tiny hand, and explained, in a voice that her father used whenever she tried to run across the street or to touch something electrical, "But I can't be your girlfriend, because I'm very smart and popular, and you're just a dirty little boy who always keeps quiet and sits far away from everyone and the only thing that's special about you is that you have glittery eyes, and even that will disappear now if I agree to be your girlfriend. Though I have to admit that today you're a lot less dirty than usual." "I mixed with water," the less-dirty little boy admitted, "to make my wish come true." "Sorry," the little girl said, running out of patience, and went back to her seat.

All that day, the little girl felt sad, because she understood that her eyes would probably never glitter. And none of the stories or the songs or the show-and-tell could make her feel any better. And every now and then, when she almost succeeded in not thinking about it, she'd see the little boy standing at the far end of the kindergarten, looking at her quietly, his eyes glittering more and more fiercely, as if out of spite.

TEDDY TRUNK

'm driving south on the old road, toward Ashdod. In the passenger seat next to me is Teddy Trunk, listening to a tape and drumming on the dashboard. He knows this road like the palm of his hand, from the time before the army, when he lived around here and used to drive to Tel Aviv with his friends every Saturday night. They're the ones who gave him that name, "Teddy Trunk." Today, no one calls him that anymore, not even just "Teddy." Today, most people call him "Mr. Schuler" or "Schuler." His wife calls him "Theodore." I don't think he really likes her to call him that.

We're on our way to a local council near Gedera to close a deal. I should probably say that he's closing a deal and I'm driving him there. That's my job. I'm a driver. I once had a route delivering dairy products; the money was better, but I just wasn't into getting up at four every morning and arguing with all those cheap-ass grocers about small change. Teddy once told me I'm a person without ambition, and that he's jealous of me because of it. I think that was the only time I felt like he was patronizing me. Most of the time, he's actually pretty all right.

On my very first day on the job, I opened the car door for him and he told me not to open doors for him, and also that he always sits in the front, even when he's reading or looking over papers. When we'd stop to eat, he always paid. I wasn't really crazy about that, and in the end we agreed that for every five times he paid, I'd pay once, because he earns about five times more than I do. That was his idea, and I said fine. It made sense to me.

The first time I treated was at a steak place in some gas station in the south. Shitty food, and the waiter, right before we paid, pegged him. "Well, what do you know. I'll be damned if it isn't Teddy Trunk." Teddy kind of smiled at the waiter and nodded, but I could tell he wasn't exactly thrilled to see him. We had an arrangement that if one of us paid, the other left the tip, and on the way out, I noticed that he didn't leave the waiter anything.

"What an asshole," I said to him later in the car. "Why? He happens to be a pretty nice guy," he said, without really meaning it, "maybe the best student in our grade. Funny he's stuck here as a waiter." I wanted to ask him about the tip, but it seemed a little out of line, so I asked about the name instead. "I don't like that name," he said instead of answering. "Don't ever call me that, OK?"

That evening, before I dropped him off, he softened up a little and told me that when he was a kid, he was once late for school. In the hallway, someone said he should tell the teacher his father drove him there and that on the way something in the car had broken down. And that's what he did. And when the teacher asked him what exactly broke down in the car, little Teddy told her that the trunk had broken down—and he was thrown out of class.

Ever since that story, even though I keep calling him "Schuler," I can't think about him with any other name but "Teddy Trunk." "I'm going to charge him such a price, that Shimshon, it'll make his yarmulke spin," Teddy says, and drums on the dashboard in time to the song on the radio. "Those guys on the local council here pretend to be hard up, but they're loaded." After his meeting, we decide to have supper in a Russian restaurant around here that's supposed to be really good. Teddy Trunk's treat. I might even have a few drinks, not too many, because I still have to drive to Tel Aviv later.

When he goes into his meeting, I park the car. The steering wheel hasn't felt right to me the whole way, and now I see that one of the front tires is almost flat. I have a spare, but the jack is gone. I might make it to Tel Aviv that way, but I have time to kill anyway. "Hey kid," I say to a skinny boy bouncing a ball in the yard, "go ask your father if he has a jack." The kid runs home and comes back with someone wearing shorts and flip-flops. "Tell me something, asshole," flip-flops says, waving his car keys at me. "Why the hell should I help you with a jack?" "Because life's happier and more fun when people are nice to each other," I say, trying a little milk-of-human-kindness on him, "and they say small-town people are nicer." "You don't remember me, do you," he says, taking his jack out of his car and tossing it to the ground near my feet. "Two pork chops, one Coke, one Diet Coke, one Bavarian cream with two spoons. Never heard of a tip, did you, Mr. Nice Guy?" And then it hits me: the guy who waited on Teddy Trunk and me. He's actually pretty nice about it, curses a little, but helps me with the tire. I've never been good with my hands. "One helluva car," he tells me when we're finished, and when I tell him that I'm only the driver, he looks surprised. "So in the restaurant, you were with your boss," he says, smiling. "Teddy Trunk—your boss? Good for him, poor guy."

His kid comes back with a family-size bottle of Coke with almost no fizz, and two glasses. "Did he ever tell you why they call him Teddy Trunk?" flip-flops asks, pouring me a glass. I nod. "What assholes we were, huh?" He laughs a pretty ugly laugh. "Do you still sometimes drive with him in the trunk, just for old times' sake?" Then, when he sees I don't understand, he tells me about how in high school, they were a gang of six, and every Saturday night they'd go to Tel Aviv together. Five in the car, and Teddy. "He used to curl up in the trunk, like this, in his going-out clothes," flip-flops says, smiling. "And we'd close the trunk and didn't open it till we got to Tel Aviv. And later, on the way back, the same thing. Did you ever ride in a trunk, all boozed up?" I shake my head. "Me neither." He takes the empty glass from me. "Well, at least now he rides in the front."

I'm driving north on the old road, toward Tel Aviv. In the passenger seat next to me is Teddy Trunk, listening to a tape and drumming on the dashboard. He knows this road like the palm of his hand, from the time before the army when he lived around here and used to drive to Tel Aviv with his friends every Saturday night. They're the ones who gave him that name, "Teddy Trunk." Today, no one calls him that anymore.

MALFFUNCTION

think my computer is ffucked up. I don't think it's the computer itselff actually, just the keyboard. I bought it not long ago, used, ffrom the classiffieds. The guy who sold it to me was weird. Opened the door wearing a silk robe and a ffedora, like some classy hooker in a black-and-white art ffilm. Made me some tea with mint that he grew in the window box. "The computer's a steal," he said. "You won't regret it." So I gave him ffive hundred, and now I do. The ad said they were selling everything because they were going on a long trip, but the guy in the ffedora gave me the real reason: he was going to drop dead any minute ffrom some disease, except that that's not something you write in an ad, especially not iff you want people to come. "The truth is," he said, "that death is kind off like a trip to somewhere, so it isn't ffalse advertising." As he said it, he had a quivery voice, optimistic, as though ffor a second he'd seen death as a ffun class trip to a new place, and not just some good-ffor-nothing darkness that's breathing down your neck. "Does it come with a warranty?" I asked, and he laughed. I was being serious, but when he laughed, I ffelt kind off weird so I pretended like I meant it as a joke.

HALIBUT

Ever since I came back to Israel, everything looks different to
me. Smelly, sad, dull. Now even those lunches with Ari that
used to light up my day are a drag. He's going to marry that
Nessia of his; today he's going to surprise me with the news. And
I, of course, will be surprised, as if Ofer the blinker hadn't told me
the secret four days ago. He loves Nessia, he'll say, and look into
my eyes. "This time," he'll say in his deep and very convincing
voice, "this time, it's real."

We made a date to meet at a fish place on the beach. The
economy's in a recession now, and the price of the lunch specials
is a joke, anything to get people in the door. Ari says the recession
is good for us, because we—though we may not have realized it
yet—are rich. Recession, Ari explains, is tough on the poor. Tough
isn't the word—it's a killer. But for the rich? It's like frequent-flier
bonus points. You can upgrade all the things you used to do and
it's free. And just like that, the Johnnie Walker goes from Red La-
bel to Black, and the four-days-plus-half-board turns into a week,
anything to get people in the door. To get their asses in the god-
damn door. "I hate this country," I tell him while we're waiting
for menus. "I'd split forever if it weren't for the business." "Get se-

rious," Ari says, putting his sandaled foot on the chair next to him. "Where else in the world can you find a beach like this?"

"In France," I tell him, "in Thailand, in Brazil, in Australia, in the Caribbean—"

"OK, OK, so go," he interrupts me smugly. "Finish your food, drink your espresso, and go!"

"I said," I stress, "that I'd go if it weren't for the business—"

"The business!" Ari bursts out laughing. "The business," he says, and waves at the waitress for a menu.

The waitress comes over to tell us what the day's specials are, and Ari gives her the uninterested look of someone in love with another girl. "And for the main dish," she says, smiling a natural, irresistible smile, "we have slices of red tuna in butter and pepper, halibut on a bed of tofu with a teriyaki sauce, and talking fish with salt and lemon." "I'll take the halibut," Ari says quickly. "What's talking fish?" I ask. "It's talking fish served raw. It's lightly salted, but not spiced—" "And it talks?" I interrupt her. "I highly recommend the halibut," the waitress continues after a nod. "I never tried the talking."

As soon as we started eating, Ari told me about marrying Nessia, or NASDAQ, as he likes to call her. He made up the name when the NASDAQ was still going up and never bothered to update it. "Congratulations," I said. "I'm glad." "Me too," Ari said, slouching a little lower in his seat. "Me too. We have a pretty good life, eh? Me and NASDAQ, you . . . alone, temporarily. A bottle of good white wine, air-conditioning, the sea."

The fish arrived fifteen minutes later. The halibut, according to Ari, was terrific. The talking—kept quiet. "So it doesn't talk," Ari snapped. "So what? Shit, don't go making a scene. I mean it, I don't have the patience." And when he saw me still waving to the waitress, he suggested, "Take a bite—if it's not good, send it back. But at least taste it first." The waitress came over with the

same irresistible smile as before. "The fish . . ." I said to her.
"Yes?" she asked, craning her already long neck. "It doesn't talk."
The waitress gave a funny little giggle and explained quickly. "The
dish is called talking fish as an indication of the kind of fish it is,
which in this case, is the kind that can talk, but the fact that it can
talk doesn't mean that it will at any given moment." "I don't understand . . ." I began. "What's to understand," the waitress said
in a condescending tone of voice. "This is a restaurant, not a
karaoke club. But if you don't like it, I'd be happy to get you
something else. You know what? I'd be happy to get you something else anyway." "I don't want something else," I insisted
pointlessly. "I want it to talk." "It's OK," Ari cut in. "You don't
have to bring anything else. Everything's great." The waitress
flashed a third identical smile and walked away. And Ari said,
"Man, I'm getting married. Do you get it? I'm marrying the love
of my life. And this time . . ." he dropped in a two-second pause,
"this time it's real. This meal, it's a celebration, so come on and
fucking eat with me. Without making a big deal about the fish
and without bellyaching about the country. Just be happy with
me, be happy with your buddy, OK?" "I'm happy," I said, "really."
"So eat that ugly fish already," he begged. "No," I said, and
quickly corrected myself. "Not yet." "Now, now," Ari urged,
"now, before it gets cold—or send it back. But I can't sit here and
watch. The fish on the table and you not talking . . ." "It's not getting cold," I corrected him. "It's raw. And I don't have to be quiet,
we can talk . . ." "OK," said Ari. "Forget it," and jumped angrily to
his feet, "I've lost my appetite anyway." He reached for his wallet,
but I stopped him. "Let it be my treat," I said without getting up,
"in honor of your wedding." "Go fuck yourself," Ari hissed, but
let go of his wallet. "Why do I even try to explain to you about
love? You homo. Did I say homo? You're not even a homo—
you're asexual . . ." "Ari . . ." I tried to interrupt him. "Even

now," Ari said, shaking a finger in the air, "even now I know that later on I'll be sorry I said that. But being sorry about it won't make it any less true." "Mazel tov," I said, trying to give him one of the waitress's natural smiles, and he gave me a half who-cares, half goodbye wave, and left.

"Is everything all right?" the waitress pantomimed from a distance. I nodded. "Your check?" she continued her pantomime. I shook my head. I looked through the window at the sea—it was a bit murky but very powerful. I looked down at the fish—lying on its stomach with its eyes closed, its body rising and falling as if it were breathing. I didn't know whether this was a smoking table, but I lit up anyway, one of those satisfying "after" cigarettes. I wasn't really hungry. It was pleasant here, looking out on the sea—too bad there was glass and air-conditioning instead of a breeze. I could sit like that looking at the sea for hours. "Take off," the fish whispered to me without opening its eyes. "Grab a cab to the airport and hop on the first plane out, it doesn't matter where to." "But I can't just take off like that," I explained in a clear, slow voice. "I have commitments here, business." The fish shut up again and so did I. Almost a minute later, it added, "Never mind, forget it. I'm depressed."

They didn't put the fish on the bill. They offered me dessert instead, and when I said no, they just subtracted forty-five shekels. "I'm sorry . . ." the waitress said, and quickly explained. "I'm sorry you didn't enjoy it." And a second later, she specified, "The fish." "No, no," I protested, dialing my cell phone for a taxi. "The fish was good. Really, you have a very nice place here."

FOR ONLY 9.99
(INC. TAX AND POSTAGE)

Nachum happened on the ad completely by chance, some-where between the daily horoscope and the sex toys. "Ever wonder about the meaning of life?" the ad inquired. "Ever ask yourself why we exist in the first place?" And it went on to provide the solution: "The answer to this difficult question is right at your fingertips. You'll find it in a small but incredible booklet. In simple and readable language you will find out why you have been placed on this earth. The booklet, printed on the finest rag stock, complete with enlightening, breathtaking color photographs, will be mailed to your home, beautifully gift-wrapped, for only 9.99!" There was a photograph of a man with glasses reading a small booklet, and smiling happily to himself. And right over his head, in the spot where his thought-bubble should have been, was the inscription, in thick lettering: "The booklet that will change your life!" Nachum was deeply impressed by the picture in the ad. The man looked very happy, and Nachum was also taken in by his broad shoulders, almost like the smiling strong-man in the ad for "The Physique of Hercules in only thirty seconds a day, with our new and improved formula. Only 9.99! (inc.

tax and postage)." To think that they were offering him the meaning of life. And at half the regular price!

Nachum's hands shook as he stuck the stamp on the envelope. He knew that the next few days would be his longest. The meaning of life was something that had worried him for as long as he could remember, and even though his life was reasonably pleasant and happy, he'd always felt there was something missing. But now, in just a few days, his world would be complete. When he tried to explain to his father the intense curiosity that was welling up within him, he encountered some resistance. "You're such a moron. Every time some two-timing swindler decides to cash in, all he needs is to place an ad, and my nincompoop of a son sends him the money." "But Dad, they're not two-timing swindlers," Nachum tried to explain. "The ad even says that if I'm not completely satisfied, I have fourteen days to send the booklet back, and they'll reimburse me. Minus the postage, of course." Nachum's dad gave a creepy snigger, and his nervous expression became downright menacing. Placing his hand on Nachum's shoulder, he whispered in a conspiratorial voice: "Know what? Let's put one over on 'em. Let's read the booklet together, and then, once we've figured out the meaning of life, we'll send it back. That'll screw them good. What do you say?" Nachum didn't say anything, though he couldn't help thinking it was very dishonest. He didn't want to upset his dad. But the vise on his shoulder was tightening. Apparently, his dad had managed to get upset all on his own. "You imbecile," he shouted. "I'll show you the meaning of life, you piece of defective goods," he ranted on, struggling to pull off his slipper. "Leave the boy alone," Nachum's mother said, rushing to his rescue, trying to separate him from his dad. "Boy?" Nachum's dad wheezed madly, waving the slipper at them as if he was about to use it.

"He'll be twenty-eight in August." "So he's a little on the naïve side," his mother whimpered. "So what?"

Nachum's friends thought it was a scam too. Even Ronit. So, having nobody to share his impatient wait with, he impatiently waited all by himself. The notice from the post office arrived three days later, and Nachum barely managed to grab it from his dad, who was about to swallow it in one of his fits of rage. As soon as he had the package in his hands, even before he'd left the post office, Nachum tore open the brown-paper wrapping and dove into the booklet on his way home. The secret of the human condition was revealed to him, becoming clearer and clearer with every page he read. The incredible booklet was written in such plain and simple language that Nachum could understand everything without having to reread it (except one part where he had to refer to the breathtaking color photographs, which really were enlightening, just as advertised). And by the time he got back to the building where he lived, he knew, for the first time in his life, why he had been placed in this wonderful world of ours, why all of us are here. And a feeling of sublime joy swept over him, a joy mingled with just a tinge of sorrow for all those years that he'd been forced to live in ignorance. Determined to ensure that others would not have to suffer the same tormenting moments of confusion, Nachum raced upstairs, and the very thought that in just a few short seconds he was about to share the secret of the human condition with his parents brought tears to his eyes—tears that were soon to turn into tears of frustration. His father screamed that he would have no part of this ridiculous farce. And while his mother did listen to his explanations, and looked at his pictures and nodded, her eyes were glazed over, and her nod lacked conviction. Clearly, she wasn't thinking about the booklet at all. She just wanted to make Nachum feel better.

The next few hours left Nachum feeling frustrated and sad. A quick glance at the newspaper was enough to remind him just how foreign the essence of the human condition was to most of humanity. All those wars, and murders, and ecological disasters— even the drops in the stock market—all those things grew out of ignorance, mistakes caused by a basic failure to understand what life was really about. Mistakes that could be corrected so easily, if only they would listen. But that was something nobody was ready to do. Not his relatives, not his friends, not even Ronit. With every fiber of his being Nachum felt the sting of disillusion- ment. But suddenly, just above the array of easy-loan ads, he caught sight of a familiar face—the man with the broad shoul- ders and the glasses. Except in this ad he was addressing a stern- looking man who seemed to be listening very closely. "People don't listen to you?" the ad asked. "Family and close friends pay no attention? We have the solution. For 9.99 we will send you a remarkable booklet, which will teach you how to win over even the most indifferent listener." Nachum could hardly contain his joy. Just as he had reached the verge of despair, everything was about to change. The time he spent waiting for the booklet was filled with eager anticipation. After four interminable days, he held the package in his hands. With bated breath he read the ed- ifying principles, and when he'd finished, he approached his dad, this time confident of success.

Matters progressed at a dizzying pace. Nachum knew the ex- istential truth, and how to get people's ear. The meaning of life was passed on by word of mouth, from one friend to another. It's hard to imagine Nachum's elation as he looked into his moth- er's glistening eyes, or listened to the delighted laughter of all his friends, especially Ronit. But complications presented them- selves. A couple of Orthodox kids, including the grandson of the rabbi of Ludvor, came to visit Nachum at his home and asked him to explain the meaning of life. Nachum was glad to oblige. He even served them some lemonade. They thanked him politely and left. Nachum didn't give it a second thought. Lots of strangers were paying him visits at that point, and those boys were no different from the rest.

But the next day hundreds of Orthodox Jews surrounded his home and filled his yard, singing religious hymns like "Son of Lilith, fear our sword—we shall prevail, so saith the Lord" and "Heathens shall be smitten." Listening to their chants, Nachum knew he was in trouble. He managed to sneak out through the bathroom window and hide in an abandoned shelter not far from his home. Every morning, Ronit would bring him some sandwiches and a thermos of coffee. She'd wrap the sandwiches in newsprint, which is how Nachum discovered that the rabbi of Ludvor's grandson had organized a mass departure of students from the yeshivas of Jerusalem, on the grounds that there was no point in seeking the truth in the sacred books, now that it was out in the open. The Orthodox community held Nachum personally responsible for the whole debacle. And as if this wasn't bad enough, his father, whose understanding of the meaning of life did not seem to have changed him much, managed to make things even worse. By finding unconventional uses for cans of baby carrots, he had sent the cantor of the Ludvor congregation into intensive care.

Nachum was keen on making the chief rabbi of the Ludvor congregation realize it was all just a misunderstanding, and to explain to him that the meaning of life as he had presented it was devoid of any antireligious implications. Quite the contrary. He himself, after all, made a point of fasting on Yom Kippur and eating matzo every Passover. He'd even received a sports bike for his bar mitzvah like any good Jewish boy. But every time he tried calling the rabbi from the phone booth on the corner, the rabbi would just mutter his *Shema Yisrael*, call out for help in Yiddish, and hang up before Nachum could say a word. Nachum was growing despondent. He was beginning to feel the effect of the persistent siege on his home and the public denunciation by the rabbis, not to mention the mildew in the shelter and his powerful craving for his mother's cooking. But it was then, just at his darkest hour, that everything changed thanks to Tuesday's tuna-fish sandwich. One of the stories in the sandwich wrapping was an interview with the Ludvor cantor, who'd been discharged after making a complete recovery from the canned-goods attack, and right above it Nachum spotted an ad. It showed the same broadshouldered guy, except that this time he was in an awkward position. Right opposite him was a bearded giant, holding a sharp ax, in a menacing pose. The guy with the glasses was giving him a piercing look, reinforced with a dotted line. The ad went like this: "Do you have any enemies? Anyone who wants to harm you? Don't worry! For 9.99 you can own our new booklet, 'Turn Enemies into Friends in Seven Easy Lessons,' and learn how to turn negative energies into positive ones with just one look!"

Nachum lost no time sending in his money, and soon the booklet arrived. He read it breathlessly, and began practicing by applying its rules to the misanthropic rats in the shelter. In no time at all, they became his friends. Nachum shaved, using the cold water of the shelter, and did his best to iron his clothes. He bought a yarmulke in the nearby used-clothing shop, and set out on his long journey to the residence of the rabbi of Ludvor. Despite his efforts to maintain a low profile, Nachum, for reasons that were not clear to him, drew a great deal of attention. When he reached the rabbi's residence, the crowd was ready for a lynching, but his friends the rats, who'd followed him around by the dozen, protected him. The rabbi came out onto the balcony to find out what was causing the commotion, and sure enough, all it took was one look from Nachum to make him realize there had been a misunderstanding. "Stop," he cried from the balcony high above. "Can't you see that you are facing the Messiah himself, and that he brings us the word of God?" And the crowd looked, and they saw. That very evening, they held a banquet. Nachum's father and the cantor of Ludvor danced together, arm in arm, as Nachum's rat friends drank themselves senseless.

From then on, it was not long before the meaning of life could be explained to the rest of humanity. The secret of human existence spread like a virus, and Nachum took the trouble to explain it personally on both of his *Nightline* appearances. Every country in the world agreed to disarm, some beating their swords into ploughshares, others finding even better applications. Nachum spent most of his time growing tomatoes in the little garden he cultivated in the backyard of his parents' apartment building, basking in the knowledge that he had played his own small part in the happiness of the entire world. There was just one thought that continued to worry him though: the thought of death. It hadn't bothered him in the past, but now that everything was so wonderful, it horrified him. Which is why Nachum was so thrilled when his father drew his attention to an ad in one of the dailies, where the broad-shouldered guy with the glasses, who was looking younger than ever, promised "a colorful booklet that will show you the way to immortality. All you need is fifteen seconds a day of exercising your sphincter muscles. For only 29.99." "Would you take a look at that?" Nachum's father grumbled. "One lucky break, and already they go and up the price."

HORSIE

The golden stick is what they call it, and you have to read the little leaflet that comes with it before your girlfriend pees on it. You make coffee, have a cookie like everything's cool, click on MTV, groove on whatever they're playing, snuggle, sing the chorus with the band. Then back to the stick. The stick has a little window. When there's one stripe in it, that means everything's OK, and when there are two—hell, you always wanted to be a father anyway.

The truth is, he loved her. But really, not that stammered sure-I-love-you kind of love. He loved her forever, like in the fairy tales, I'd-walk-down-the-aisle-tomorrow kind of love, except that the whole business with the baby really stressed him out. It was pretty heavy stuff for her too, but an abortion was even scarier. And if they knew they were heading toward a family anyway, so it was just pushing up the schedule. "You're freaking out." She laughed. "Look how you're sweating." "Sure I'm freaking out," he said, trying to laugh too. "It's easy for you, you have a uterus, but me, you know me, I get uptight even when there's no reason and now that there is . . ." "I'm scared too," she said, wrapping herself around him. "Forget it," he said, and hugged her. "It'll all work out in the end, you'll see. If it's a boy,

I'll teach him how to play soccer, and if it's a girl—you know what, it wouldn't hurt her either." Then she cried a little and he comforted her, and then she fell asleep and he didn't. Far back, deep inside him, he could feel his hemorrhoids opening one by one like flowers in springtime.

At first, when there was no belly yet, he tried not to think about it, not that it helped, but at least it gave him something to aim for. Later, when she started to show a little, he began to imagine it sitting there in her stomach, a pocket-size little asshole in a shiny three-piece suit. And really, how could he know that it wouldn't be born a little shit, because kids, they're like Russian roulette, you never know in advance what you'll end up with. Once, when she was in her third month, he went to the mall to buy something for his computer and saw a disgusting kid in overalls forcing his mother to buy him a video game, pretending he'd haul his chubby little body over the second-floor railing if she didn't. "Jump," he shouted at the kid from below. "I dare you, you little blackmailing shit," and took off before the hysterical mother could sic the security guards on him. The next night, he dreamed he was pushing his girlfriend down the steps so she'd have a miscarriage. Or maybe it wasn't a dream, just a thought that went through his mind when they went out to the movies, and he started thinking this was no joke. He had to do something. Something serious, not on the level of a conversation with his mother, or even with his grandmother. This called for nothing less than a visit to his great-grandmother.

His great-grandmother was so old it was depressing, and if there was something she hated, it was visitors. She spent the whole day at home OD'ing on soap operas, and if she did let someone come to visit, she refused to turn off the TV. "I'm scared, Great-grandmother," he blubbered on the living room couch. "I'm so scared, you have no idea." "Of what?" the great-grandmother asked, still watching some mustachioed Victor who'd just told a woman wrapped in a towel that he was actually her father. "I don't know," he mumbled. "Maybe something I never wanted will be born." "Listen to me carefully, Great-grandson," said the great-grandmother, nodding her head in time to the closing music of the series. "At night, wait till she falls asleep, and then lie with your head right up against her belly, so that all your dreams move straight into it." He nodded, even though he didn't really understand, but the great-grandmother explained, "A dream is nothing but a strong wish. So strong that you can't even put it into words. Now, the fetus, which is in her belly, has no opinions about anything, so he'll sop it right up. Whatever you dream, that's exactly what will be."

After that, he slept every night with his head right next to her belly, which was getting bigger all the time. He didn't remember the dreams, but he was willing to swear they were good ones. And he couldn't remember a time in his life when he'd slept that way, so peacefully, he didn't even get up to pee. His wife didn't really understand that funny position she found him in every morning, but was happy to see him relaxed again and he stayed relaxed the whole way, right to the delivery room. Not that he didn't care or anything like that—he was very much into it—it was just that his fears had been replaced by anticipation. And even when he saw the obstetrician and the nurses whispering together before the doctor walked reluctantly over to him, he never lost confidence that everything would be fine.

In the end, they had a little horse. More accurately, a pony. They called him Hemi, after a successful industrialist whose glitzy TV appearances had impressed the great-grandmother, and they raised him with lots of love. On Saturdays, they rode him to the park and played all kinds of games with him, mainly cowboys and Indians. The truth is that after the birth, she was depressed for a long time, and even though they never talked about it, he knew that no matter how much she loved Hemi, deep in her heart, she wanted something different.

Meanwhile, in the soap opera, the woman in the towel shot Victor, twice, making the great-grandmother very unhappy. (He'd been hooked up to a respirator for quite a few episodes now.) At night, after everyone fell asleep, he'd turn off the TV and go to look at Hemi, who slept on the hay he'd spread on the floor of the nursery. Hemi was very funny when he slept, shaking his head from side to side as if he were listening to someone talking to him, and every once in a while, he even whinnied at some especially funny dream. She took Hemi to a lot of specialists, who said he would never really grow. "He'll stay a midget," as she'd put it, but Hemi wasn't a midget, he was a pony. "Too bad," he'd whisper every night when he put him to sleep, "too bad Mom couldn't dream a dream that might've come true, too." And then he'd stroke Hemi's mane and hum him a medley of children's and horses' songs, a medley that always opened with "All the Pretty Little Ponies" and ended only when he himself fell asleep.

MY GIRLFRIEND'S
NAKED

Outside, the sun's shining, and downstairs on the lawn, my girlfriend's naked. June twenty-first, the longest day of the year. People walking past our building look at her, some even find a reason to stop—they have to tie their shoelaces, let's say, or they stepped on some shit and absolutely have to scrape it off their shoes this very instant. But some of them stop without an excuse, real straight-shooters. Before, one of them even whistled, but my girlfriend didn't notice because she'd just come to a gripping passage in her book. And the guy who whistled waited for a second, but when he saw her keep on reading, he left. She reads a lot, my girlfriend, but never like that, outside, naked. And I'm sitting on our balcony on the third floor, front, trying to figure out how I feel about it. I'm a little off when it comes to that knowing-how-I-feel thing. Sometimes, friends come over on Saturday night and get all worked up, arguing about all kinds of things. Once, someone even got up in the middle, mad as hell, and went home. And I just sit there with them and watch TV with the sound off and read the subtitles. Sometimes, in the heat of an argument, someone may ask me what I think. And then, most of the time, I pretend like I'm thinking, finding it hard to put my thoughts into words, and there's always someone who takes advantage of the silence to jump in with his two cents.

But there, we're talking about more general subjects, politics and stuff, and here, this is my girlfriend we're talking about, and she's naked. Really, I tell myself, I should know how I feel about that. Now the Elizovs come out the front door where the intercom is. The Elizovs live two floors above us, the penthouse. The man's very old, maybe a hundred. I don't even know his first name, just that it starts with an "S," and that he's an engineer, because next to their regular mailbox there's another one, bigger, that has S. Elizov, Engineer, written on it, and it can't be her, because our neighbor across the hall once told me that she's a customs inspector. She's no spring chicken either, Mrs. Elizov, and her blond hair is right out of a bottle. The first time we rode in the elevator with them, my girlfriend was sure she was a call girl because her perfume had a smell kind of like detergent. The Elizovs stop and look at my girlfriend naked on the lawn. They're the two most influential people on the tenants' committee. The climbing vine on the fence, for example, was their idea. Mr. Elizov whispers something into his wife's ear, she shrugs, and they keep on walking. My girlfriend doesn't even notice them go past her, she's so caught up in her book, so engrossed. And what I feel, if I really try to put it into words, is that it's great that she's getting a tan, because when she's tan, it makes the green of her eyes stand out. And if she's going to get a tan, then the best way is naked, because if there's one thing I hate, it's those bathing-suit strap marks, when everything's dark and all of a sudden, white. It always makes you feel that it's not even the same skin, that it's some synthetic thing you buy at Club Med. On the other hand, it's not such a good idea to piss off the Elizovs. Because we're only renting the place and we do have the option to stay for two years, but still. If they start saying we're causing problems, the landlord could throw us out with sixty days' notice. It says so in the lease. Even though that on-the-other-hand has nothing to do with anybody's feelings on the subject, definitely not mine, it's more like a kind of risk we have to consider. My girlfriend's turning on her back now. Her ass is my absolute favorite, but her tits are something too. A kid going by on his Rollerblades yells at her, "Hey, lady, your cunt is showing!" As if she didn't know. My brother once said she's the kind of girl who doesn't stay in one place very long, and I should be prepared so she won't break my heart. That was a long time ago, I think, almost two years. And when that guy down there whistled at her, all of a sudden I remembered that, and for a second, I was scared she'd get up and leave.

The sun'll be going down soon, and she'll come back inside. Because there won't be any more light for sunbathing, or for reading either. And when she does come in, I'll slice us some watermelon and we'll eat it on the balcony, together. If she comes up soon, maybe we'll even get to see the sunset.

BOTTLE

Two guys are sitting together in a bar. One of them is majoring in something or other in college, the other abuses his guitar once a day and thinks he's a musician. They've already had two beers, and they're planning to have at least two more. The college guy just happens to be depressed because he's in love with his roommate, and the roommate has a hairy-necked boyfriend who sleeps over at their apartment every night, and in the morning, when they accidentally bump into each other in the kitchen, he makes you-have-my-sympathy faces at the college guy, and that only depresses him more. "Move out," the guy who thinks he's a musician tells him—this musician guy, he has a history of avoiding conflict. All of a sudden, in the middle of the conversation, some drunk with a ponytail they've never seen before comes in and asks the college student if he'd bet a hundred shekels that he can put his friend, the musician, into a bottle. The college guy says yes right away, because, really, the bet sounds pretty dumb, and in a second, the ponytail puts the musician into an empty Carlsberg bottle. The college guy doesn't have much money to spare, but fair is fair, he takes out the hundred shekels, pays up, and goes back to staring at the wall and feeling sorry for himself. "Tell him," his friend shouts from the bottle. "Come on, quick, before he goes." "Tell him what?" the college guy asks. "To get me out of the bottle now, come on," but by the time the college guy gets the message, the ponytail has split. So he pays, takes his best friend in the bottle, hails a cab, and together, they go looking for the ponytail. One thing's for sure, that ponytail didn't look like someone who got drunk by mistake; he's a pro. So they go from bar to bar. And at each one, they have another drink, so they won't feel like they wasted their time. The college guy downs them in a single gulp, and the more he drinks, the sorrier he feels for himself. The guy in the bottle drinks through a straw. It's not as if he has too many options.

At five in the morning, when they find the ponytail in a bar near the beach, they're both wasted. The ponytail is wasted too, and he feels really bad about the bottle thing. Right away, he says he's sorry and takes the musician out of the bottle. He's really embarrassed about forgetting the guy inside, so he buys another round for them, their last. They talk a little, and the ponytail tells them that he learned the bottle trick from a Finnish guy he met in Thailand. It turns out that in Finland that trick is considered kid stuff. And ever since, every time the ponytail goes out drinking and is stuck without cash, he gets hold of some by betting. And the ponytail even teaches them how to do the trick, that's how bad he feels. The truth? Once you catch on, you're amazed how easy it is.

By the time the college guy gets home, the sun is almost up. And before he can even try to get his key in the lock, the door opens, and there's hairy-neck, standing in front of him, all showered and shaved. Before hairy-neck starts to go down the stairs, he manages to toss his girlfriend's drunk roommate an I-know-you-went-out-to-get-crocked-only-because-of-her look. And the college guy crawls quietly to his room, managing to get a peek at his roommate—Sivan, that's her name—sleeping under the covers in her room with her mouth half open, like a baby. She has this special kind of beauty now, serene. The kind of beauty people have only when they're sleeping, but not all of them. And for a minute, he feels like taking her, just the way she is, putting her in a bottle and keeping her next to his bed, like those bottles of multicolored sand people used to bring back from the Sinai. Like the small night-lights you keep on for kids who are afraid to sleep alone in the dark.

A VISIT TO THE COCKPIT

When we landed in Tel Aviv, the whole airplane burst into applause and I started to cry. My father, who was sitting in the aisle seat, tried to calm me down, and at the same time, explain to anyone who was polite enough to listen that this was the first time I'd ever flown abroad, and that's why I was a little emotional. "When we took off, she was actually fine," he blabbered to an old man with Coke-bottle glasses who stank of piss, "and now, after landing, all of a sudden she's letting it out." In the same breath, he put a hand on the back of my neck, the way you do with a dog, and whispered in a syrupy voice, "Don't cry, sweetie, Daddy's here." I wanted to kill him, I wanted to hit him so hard he'd bleed. But Daddy kept on kneading the back of my neck, whispering loudly to the smelly old man that I'm not usually like this, and that I'd been an artillery instructor in the army, and that my boyfriend, Giora, how ironic, is even a security officer for El Al.

A week before, when I landed in New York, my boyfriend, Giora, how ironic, was waiting for me with flowers right at the door of the plane. He works at the airport, so that was easy to arrange. We kissed on the steps, like in some Hallmark movie, and he whisked me and my suitcases through passport control in a second. From the airport, we drove straight to a restaurant that overlooks all of Manhattan. He'd bought an '88 Cadillac, but it was so clean it looked new. In the restaurant, Giora didn't really know what to order, and we finally settled on something with a funny name that looked a little like an octopus and smelled awful. Giora tried to eat it and to say it was good, but after a few seconds, he gave up too, and we both started laughing. He'd grown a beard since I saw him last, and it actually looked good on him. From the restaurant, we went to the Statue of Liberty and MoMA, and I pretended to love it, but I had this weird feeling the whole time. I mean, we hadn't seen each other for more than two months, and instead of going to his place and fucking or just sitting and talking a little, we're schlepping around to these tourist attractions that Giora must have seen at least two hundred times, and he's giving me these tired explanations of every single one. In the evening, when we got to his apartment, he said he had a phone call to make, and I went to take a shower. I was still drying myself off, and he'd already cooked a pot of spaghetti and set the table with wine and the half-dead flowers. I really wanted us to talk. I don't know, I had this feeling that something bad had happened and he didn't want to tell me, like in those movies when someone dies and they try to hide it from the children. But Giora kept yakking away about all the places he had to show me in a week, about how he was afraid we wouldn't see them all because the city's so big, and it isn't really a week, barely five days, because one day was over already and on the last day, I was flying in the evening, and my father was coming into town before that, so we definitely couldn't do anything. I stopped him with a kiss; I couldn't think of any other way. The bristles of his beard scratched my face a little. "Giora," I asked, "is everything all right?"

"Sure," he said, "sure, it's just that we have so little time, and I'm afraid we won't get to see anything."

The spaghetti was actually very good, and after we fucked, we sat on the balcony, drank some wine, and looked at all the teeny-tiny people walking past on the street. I said to Giora that it must be really exciting to live in such a huge city, that I could sit on the balcony like that for hours just watching all those little dots below, trying to guess what they were thinking about. And Giora said, "You get used to it," and went to get himself a Diet Coke. "You know," he said, "only last night I was about ten blocks west of here, where all the hookers are. You can't see it from here, it's on the other side of the building. And some older homeless guy comes up to the car—he actually looked okay for a homeless guy. His clothes were old and everything, and he had one of those supermarket carts full of paper bags, the kind they always drag around from place to place, but except for that, he looked completely sane, sort of clean. It's hard to explain. And that homeless guy came up to me and offered to give me a blow job for ten bucks. 'I'll do it real good,' he said to me. 'I'll swallow every drop.' And all in a kind of businesslike tone, like someone offering to sell you a TV. I didn't know what to do with myself. You know, two in the morning, a line of twenty Puerto Rican hookers standing twenty yards from him, some of them really pretty, and this guy, who looks exactly like my uncle, is offering to give me a blow job. Then it hit him too, it must have been the first time he'd ever offered to do such a thing, and all of a sudden, we were both embarrassed. And he said to me, half apologizing, 'So maybe I can wash your car instead? Five bucks. I'm really hungry.' And that's how I found myself in the grungiest part of Manhattan, two in the morning, a guy about forty washing my car with a bottle of mineral water and a rag that used to be a Chicago Bulls T-shirt. Some of the hookers started walking toward us, and a black guy too, who looked like their pimp, and I was sure things were going to get ugly, but none of them said a word. They just looked at us without saying anything. And when the guy finished, I said thank you, paid, and drove away."

Neither of us said anything after that story. I looked at the sky, and it seemed very black all of a sudden. I asked him what he was doing on a street of hookers in the middle of the night, and he said that wasn't the point. I asked him if he had someone, and he didn't answer that either. I asked him if she was a hooker. At first, he didn't say anything, then he said she worked for Lufthansa. Now I could suddenly sense her smell on him, coming from his body, his beard. A little like the smell of sauerkraut, and now, after we'd fucked, that smell was clinging to me too. He insisted that I stay in his apartment for the week anyway, and I immediately said yes; I didn't have much choice. There was only one bed, and I didn't want to be a bitch, so we slept in it together, but we didn't have sex. I knew I would never fuck him again, and he knew it too. After he fell asleep, I went to take another shower, to wash her smell off me, even though I knew that as long as I slept in the same bed with him, the smell would linger.

On the day of the flight, I wore my nicest clothes so Giora would get a little taste of what he was missing, but I don't think he even noticed. I was really happy when we went to meet my father at the hotel. I gave him a big hug, and that surprised him a little, but you could see how happy he was. My father asked Giora a few stupid questions, and Giora squirmed a little, saying he had somewhere he needed to go, and he was sorry he couldn't drive us to the airport. Then he went to get my suitcases from the car and as we said goodbye and pretended to kiss, my father couldn't tell anything was wrong. When Giora was gone, I went up to my father's room and showered again, and my father called for a cab to take us to the airport. During the flight, I was very quiet, and he talked the whole time. That week had passed so slowly for me, and to cheer myself up, I'd tell myself this was my last Monday here, or my last Tuesday, just like I did in the last week of basic training, only this time it didn't really help. And even now, with the nightmare finally over, I didn't feel any relief. Even the smell of her was still there. I sniffed myself, trying to figure out where it was coming from, and suddenly I realized it was from my watch. Her smell had stayed on my watch from the very first night.

After the meal, my father pretended he was going to the bathroom and came back with a flight attendant. That's when it dawned on me that he'd arranged a surprise visit to the cockpit. I was such a wreck I didn't even have the strength to argue with him. I dragged myself behind the flight attendant to the cockpit, where the pilot and the navigator explained all kinds of boring things to me about the instruments and the switches. Finally, the pilot, who had gray hair, asked how old I was, and the navigator burst out laughing. The pilot gave him a murderous look, and he stopped and apologized. "I didn't mean anything," he said. "I'm just used to, you know, mostly kids coming in here." The pilot said that, in any case, it was very nice of me to visit them in the cockpit and asked if I'd had a good time in New York. I said yes. The pilot said he was crazy about that city, because it had everything. And the navigator, who probably felt a little uncomfortable and wanted to say something too, said that he personally had a little problem with the poverty you see there, but today, with all the Russian immigrants, you actually see it in Israel too. After that, they asked me if I'd gotten to eat in that new restaurant that overlooks all of Manhattan, and I said yes. When I went back, my father was beaming and he changed places with me so I could see the landing better. As I tried to push my seat into a reclining position, he rubbed the back of my hand and said, "Sweetheart, the red light's on, you'd better fasten your seat belt. We're going to land in a jiffy." And I fastened my seat belt real tight and felt how, in a jiffy, I was going to cry.

A THOUGHT IN THE
SHAPE OF A STORY

This is a story about people who once lived on the moon. Nowadays, there's no one up there, but up until just a few years ago, the place was mobbed. The people on the moon thought they were very special, because they could think their thoughts in any shape they wanted. In the shape of a pot, or a table, even in the shape of flared pants. So people on the moon could bring their girlfriend an original present, like an I-love-you thought in the shape of a coffee mug or an I'll-always-be-true thought in the shape of a vase.

It was very impressive, all those shaped thoughts, except that as time passed, the people on the moon came to a kind of agreement about how every thought should look. A mother-love thought should always be shaped like a curtain, while a father-love thought was shaped like an ashtray, so that it didn't matter what house you walked into, you could always guess what thoughts in what shape would be waiting there arranged on the tea trolley in the living room.

Of all the people on the moon, there was one who shaped his thoughts differently. He was a young guy, a little strange, and most of the time he was troubled by existential, more or less irritating, questions. The main thought going through his mind was the kind that believes every person has at least one unique thought resembling only itself and him. A thought with color and volume and content which only that person could have.

This guy's dream was to build a spaceship, sail around space in it, and collect all the unique thoughts. He didn't go to social events, he hardly went out at all, he spent all his time building the spaceship. He built the engine in the shape of a thought of wonder, and the steering system in the shape of a thought of pure logic, and that was only the beginning. He added lots of other sophisticated thoughts that would help him navigate and survive in outer space, but his neighbors, who watched him while he worked, saw that he was constantly making mistakes. Because only someone who really had no idea could create a thought of curiosity in the shape of an engine, when it was absolutely clear that a thought like that had to look like a microscope. Not to mention that a thought of pure logic, unless you want it to look tacky, has to be shaped like a shelf. They tried to explain but he wouldn't listen. His desire to find all the true thoughts in the universe went beyond the bounds of good taste, not to mention sanity.

One night, when the guy was sleeping, a few of his neighbors on the moon got together and, because they felt sorry for him, they broke the nearly completed spaceship down into the various thoughts he'd used to make it, and rearranged them. When the young guy got up in the morning, he found shelves, vases, thermoses, and microscopes where his spaceship had been. The whole pile was covered with a thought of sorrow—in the shape of an embroidered tablecloth—about his beloved dog who'd died.

The young guy was not at all happy about the surprise. And instead of saying thank you, he went crazy, started carrying on and breaking things. The people on the moon watched him, stunned. They really did not like that sort of behavior. The moon, as you know, is a planet with very little gravitational force. And the smaller a planet's gravitational force is, the more dependent it is on discipline and order, because it takes only a little push for objects to lose their equilibrium. And if everyone who felt even slightly bitter started carrying on, it would end in disaster. Finally, when they saw that the guy wasn't about to calm down, they had no choice but to think of a way to stop him. So they thought one thought of loneliness that was about three-by-three, and put him inside it, a thought the size of a cell with a very low ceiling. And every time he accidentally touched one of the sides, he felt a kind of cold blast that reminded him of his solitude.

It was in that cell that he thought a last thought of despair in the shape of a rope, tied a noose, and hanged himself. The people on the moon were so excited about the idea of a rope of despair with a noose on one end that they immediately thought despair thoughts of their own and wound them around their necks. And that's how all the people on the moon became extinct, leaving behind only that cell of loneliness. But after a hundred years of space storms, that collapsed too.

When the first spaceship reached the moon, the astronauts couldn't find anyone around. All they found was a million craters. At first, the astronauts thought those craters were ancient graves of people who had once lived on the moon. Only on closer inspection did they discover that those craters were merely thoughts about nothing.

GUR'S THEORY OF BOREDOM

Of all my friends, my friend Gur has the most theories. And of all his theories, the one that definitely has the best chance of being right is his theory of boredom. According to Gur's theory of boredom, everything that happens in the world today is because of boredom: love, war, inventions, fake fireplaces—ninety-five percent of all that is pure boredom. He includes in the other five percent, for example, the time two guys beat the shit out of him when they robbed him on the subway in New York two years ago. Not that those two guys weren't a little bored, but they looked really hungry. He likes to explain this theory of his at the beach, when he's too tired to play paddleball or go into the water. And I sit and listen for the thousandth time, secretly hoping that this is the day a gorgeous woman will walk up to where we're sitting. Not that we'd try to hit on her or anything, just so there'd be something to look at.

The last time I heard Gur's theory was a week ago, when some plainclothes cop caught us on Ben Yehuda Street with a shoebox full of grass. "Most laws come from boredom too," Gur explained to them in the back of the patrol car, "which is totally cool. It makes things interesting. People who break the law are uptight about getting caught, which helps them pass the time. And the police—the police really have a ball. Because everybody knows that time flies when you're enforcing the law. That's why, in principle, I have no problem with your arresting us. There's just one thing I can't quite understand: Why the handcuffs?"

"Shut the fuck *up*," barked the plainclothes cop with the sunglasses who was sitting in back with us. You could tell he wasn't exactly thrilled to be busting two assclowns for smoking up because they ran out of money for beer, when he could have been hauling in some serial rapist or terrorist, or even just an everyday bank robber.

Gur and I really dug the interrogation. Not only did they have AC, there was this cute lady cop who sat with us for a few hours and even made us some coffee in Styrofoam cups, and Gur explained his theory on the war between the sexes to her and got her to laugh at least twice. In fact, the whole thing was pretty laid-back except for one slightly freaky moment, when a cop who'd seen too many *NYPD Blue* episodes came into the room in the middle and wanted to slap us around. But we played it smart and confessed to everything before he could even get close. Now, when I tell only the interesting parts, it probably sounds as if it all happened very fast, but the truth is that by the time they got done filling out all the forms, it was after dark. Gur called Orit, who'd been his girlfriend for almost eight straight years and only just wised up enough six months ago to leave him and find herself a guy who was more together, and she came right down to the station to post our bail. She came alone, without her boyfriend, pretending to be pissed off that here was Gur, dragging her back into one of his lame situations. But you could tell how happy she was to see him and how much she'd missed him. After she sprang us, Gur wanted to go get some coffee or something with her, but she said she had to run, because she was working the night shift at the Super-Pharm. Maybe another time. And Gur told her that he'd been calling and leaving her messages of love but she never called him back, and if he hadn't been arrested he never would've seen her at all, and she said it would be better if he didn't call, because nothing good would ever come of their being together, or of him either, as long as he kept hanging out with guys like me and did nothing but eat shwarma, smoke joints, and look at girls. And I didn't mind when she talked that way about me, because she actually meant it in a kind of friendly way. Besides, it was true. "I really am late," she said, and got into her Beetle. And as she'd pulled away, she even waved goodbye through the window.

Then we walked all the way home from the police station on Dizengoff Street without talking, which is pretty normal for me but really unusual for Gur. "Tell me," I said to him when we got to my block. "That boyfriend of Orit's, you want us to beat the shit out of him?" "Forget it," Gur mumbled. "He's all right." "I know he's all right," I told him, "but still, if you want, we can beat the shit out of him." "No," Gur said, "but I think I'll take your bike and ride over to look at Orit for a while at the Super-Pharm." "Sure," I said, and gave him the key.

That was one of his regular pastimes, going to look at Orit when she worked nights. And, honestly, if you look at it theoretically, hiding behind a bush for five hours to watch someone ring things up on a cash register and put aspirin and Q-tips in bags really would be something you'd do out of boredom, except somehow, when it came to Orit, those theories of Gur's never seemed to work.

THE TITS ON AN EIGHTEEN-YEAR-OLD

There's nothing like the tits on an eighteen-year-old," the cabdriver said, and honked at a girl who didn't know better than to turn around. "Believe me, you sink your teeth into one or two of those a day, your bald spot disappears." Then he laughed and touched the place on his head where he once had hair. "Don't get me wrong. Me, I got two kids that age. And if I ever caught my daughter with some old fart my age—I don't know what I'd do to her. But that's the way it is, that's nature, that's how God created us, right? So tell me, why should I be ashamed? There, just look at that one," he said, honking at a girl with a Walkman who didn't stop. "How old would you say she was? Sixteen? And look at that ass. Tell me the truth, wouldn't you like a piece of that?" He honked another few times before giving up. "Doesn't hear a thing, that one," he explained, "because of the tape. I mean come on, after you see one like that, how can you go back to your wife." "You're married?" I asked, trying to sound accusing. I wished I hadn't taken the front seat. "Divorced," the driver mumbled, and tried to keep a little more of the girl with the Walkman in the rearview mirror. "Believe me, how can you even think about going back to the wife."

There was a sad song on the radio, and the driver, who was trying to sing along with it, was too happy to stick with the beat. He switched to a different station, where another sad song was waiting. "It's because of all that shit with the helicopters," he explained to me, as if I'd just landed from Mars, "those helicopters that crashed in midair. Did you hear about it? They announced it before, on the news." I nodded. "Now they're gonna kill our shifts for us. I swear, nothing but bad news and sad songs." At a pedestrian crossing, he stopped for a tall young girl wearing a back brace. "She's not bad either, huh?" he said, hesitating a little. "Give her maybe another year or two." And then he honked at her too, just to be on the safe side. He kept switching radio stations, and stopped on one that was reporting from the site of the crash. "Take me, for example," he said. "I got a kid in the army now, in a combat unit. Haven't heard from him in two days. So if I say you gotta put something lighter on the radio when these disasters happen, nobody would say I was wrong, right? What I'm saying is, they're getting us all worked up for nothing. Think about his mother, my ex. She's gotta listen to all those songs about soldiers going on about how their buddy died in their arms. What she needs is something to take the edge off. Come on," he said, suddenly touching my hand, "let's call her, yank her chain a little." I didn't answer. I was taken aback when he touched me.

"Hey, Rona, howya doin'?" he was already yelling into the speaker phone. "Everything OK?" He winked at me and gestured toward a peroxide in a beat-up Subaru Justy standing next to us at the light. "I'm worried about Yossi," a slightly metallic voice replied from the other end. "He didn't call." "How can he call? He's in the army, in the field. What, you think they got pay phones at the front?" "I don't know," the woman said. "I have a bad feeling." "You're really something, you and your feelings," the driver said, winking at me again. "I was just saying to this fare I got how, if I know you, you're worrying." "Why? You aren't worried?" "No," the driver said, laughing. "And you know why? Because I'm not like you. I listen to what they actually say on the radio, not just those tear-jerkers in the middle. And what they say is that the ones in the helicopters were paratroopers, and our Yossi isn't a paratrooper, so what's to worry?" "They said *also* paratroopers," Rona mumbled. "That doesn't mean there weren't others." Even though the connection was bad, I could hear her crying. "Do me a favor, there's this hotline for parents. Call them and ask about him. For me." "Didn't I just tell you?" the driver insisted. "They said *paratroopers*. I'm not gonna call now like some kind of schmuck." And when he didn't get an answer from the other end, he went on: "You wanna look like a retard? So you call." "OK," she said, trying to sound tough. "So get off the line." "Well, listen to you!" the driver said, and hung up. "Now she'll even spend ten hours trying to get through, anything, just so they check it for her," he said, and gave a short, empty laugh. "Real stubborn, that one, don't listen to no one."

He was looking through the windshield for something to honk at, but the streets were almost deserted. "Believe me," he said, "an ugly young girl is better than a beautiful old broad, and I'm talking from experience. A young one, even if she's ugly, her skin's still tight, her tits stand up, her body has a kinda smell, young. I'm telling you, there are lots of beautiful things in the world, but the body of a seventeen, eighteen-year-old girl . . ." He tried to hum a different song from the one on the radio, and after two verses, the car phone rang. "That's her." He smiled at me and winked again. "Rona, honey," he said, and moved his face closer to the speaker phone, as if he were a radio broadcaster flirting with his listeners. "How are you?" "Fine," the woman answered in a happy voice, making an effort to sound formal. "I just called to tell you they said he's OK." "Is that what you're calling for?" The driver laughed. "You dummy, I already told you fifteen minutes ago he was OK, didn't I?" "You did," she sighed, "but now I feel better." "So good for you," he said, trying to be sarcastic. "OK, I'm going to sleep. I'm dead tired." "Sweet dreams," the driver said, putting his finger on the button that disconnects the car phone, "and next time, listen to me, huh?" We were very close to my house now, and pulling into Reiness Street, he saw a thin girl in a miniskirt who turned around, frightened, when he honked. "Get a load of that one," he said, trying to hide his tears. "Say, wouldn't you like to stick it to her?"

BWOKEN

For Yaniv he brought a toy monkey wearing a peaked cap. When you pressed the monkey's back, it made a strange growling sound, stuck out a long tongue that reached its nose, and crossed its eyes. Dafna thought it was an ugly toy and that Yaniv would be afraid of it. But Yaniv actually seemed delighted. "Huaaah!" he'd growl, trying to imitate the monkey. He couldn't cross his eyes, so he blinked instead, then he laughed with pleasure. There's something so perfect about a child's enjoyment that nothing can compete with it. And in Daddy-Avner's present state of mind, he wasn't offering much competition.

For Dafna he brought some perfume—she'd written the name on a piece of paper for him—from the duty-free shop. There'd been a small bottle and a large one, and he bought the large one without hesitating. When it came to money, Husband-Avner was never stingy. "I asked for eau de toilette," Dafna said. "That's what my note said." "And . . . ?" he asked impatiently. "It doesn't matter," Dafna said, with a bitter smile that said exactly the opposite. "You bought perfume. It's a little strong for me, but it's great too."

For his mother, he brought a carton of Kent Longs. His mother was easy when it came to gifts. "I want you to know that I'm very worried about Yaniv," she said, ripping the cellophane wrapper off the carton of cigarettes. "What's wrong with Yaniv?" Son-Avner asked in the indifferent tone of someone who knows who he's dealing with. "At the pediatric clinic they said he's short for his age, and when he gets hit, he doesn't hit back, but that's not—" "What do you mean, 'when he gets hit'? Somebody hit him?" "I hit him, a little, not really hit, push, to teach him to defend himself. But all he does is curl up in a corner and scream. I'm telling you, next year he's going to nursery school, and if he doesn't learn how to defend himself by then, the other children will chew him up alive." "No one's going to do any chewing," he said, raising his voice. "And you, stop being a hysterical grandmother." "All right, all right," his mother said, pouting, and lit a cigarette. "But if you'd let me finish, you would've heard that I said myself that wasn't the half of it. What I really find hard to take is that the child doesn't know how to say 'Daddy.' Did you ever hear of a child who doesn't know how to say 'Daddy'? And it's not that he doesn't talk. He knows lots of words—'cookie,' 'baby,' 'cat,' you name it; only 'Daddy' he doesn't know, and if it weren't for me, he wouldn't have learned 'Nana' either." "He doesn't call me 'Daddy.' He calls me by a nickname instead," he said, trying to smile. "You don't have to blow it all out of proportion." "Excuse me, Avner, but 'Hello!' is not a nickname, 'Hello!' is what you shout into the phone when you can't hear. You know, he calls Aviv, your downstairs neighbor, by his name, but when it comes to his own father, he yells 'Hello!' Like you're some hooligan who stole his parking spot."

"This country is like a woman," Businessman-Avner said to the German investor in labored English, "beautiful, dangerous, unpredictable—that's part of its magic. I wouldn't exchange it for any other place in the world." As often happened, he wasn't certain if what he was saying was really true. Maybe it was, but one thing was for sure, it worked much better with investors than the other kinds of thoughts, the frightening ones that go through his mind. "This country is the black under the fingernails of the Western world—thinks it's Europe, but it's nothing more than a lump of sweat and dirt that's developed a consciousness." No, words like those don't earn you dividends. "Now, tell me the truth, Herman," he said, smiling, and handed his credit card to the tastefully tattooed waitress. "Is there anyplace in Frankfurt where the sushi's as good as this?"

After he came, they stayed in the same position. She was kneeling on all fours and he was bending over her. They didn't move, and they didn't say anything either, as if they were afraid of spoiling this good accidental thing. When he got tired, he leaned his head on her shoulder and closed his eyes. "We're good," Dafna whispered, as if to herself, but actually for him. And he felt cheated. Let her say she's good, Lover-Avner thought, why does she insist on dragging me into it too, taking over, calling it by name. His eyes stayed closed; he could feel her slide out from under his body, his own body sinking into the mattress. "We're good together," she took the trouble to specify, and ran her hand along his spine in a half-medical movement, as if measuring the distance between his brainstem and the tip of his prick. He kept on digging into the mattress. "Say something," she whispered in his ear. "What?" he asked. "It doesn't matter," she whispered. "Anything." "Don't you think it's strange that he doesn't know how to say 'Daddy'?" he asked, turning his gaze to her. "You know, he can even say 'apple' already, and the names of half the people in the building." "I don't think it's strange at all," Dafna said, going back to her regular, businesslike voice. "He calls you 'Hello!' and you come—so he thinks your name is 'Hello!' If it bothers you, correct him." "It doesn't really bother me," he muttered. "I'm just wondering if it's normal."

In the evening, Spectator-Avner sat in front of the TV and

watched Yaniv, who was playing with his toy monkey, which, for some reason, had stopped growling. "Hello!" Yaniv shouted at him, waving the toy monkey. "Hello!" "Daddy," Daddy-Avner whispered pleadingly, his voice almost inaudible. "Hello!" Yaniv insisted, shaking the monkey violently. "Bwoken!" "Say 'Daddy' and I'll fix it," Businessman-Avner said with surprising sharpness. "Hello!" Yaniv yelled. "Hel-l-l-o-o-o! Bwo-o-o-ken!" Avner didn't cave. "It's up to you. Either 'Hello!' and 'Bwoken,' or 'Daddy' and 'Huaaah!'" Yaniv listened to Businessman-Avner imitating the monkey's growl, froze for an instant, then burst out laughing. At first, Person-Avner thought the laughter was scornful, but a minute later, he could see that it was nothing more than true happiness. "Huaaah!" Yaniv laughed, left the toy monkey on the floor, and began walking toward him in determined, though not altogether steady, steps. "Huaaah! Hello!" "Huaaah!" Daddy-Hello growled, and swung the laughing Yaniv in the air. "Huaaaaah!"

BABY

On his twenty-ninth birthday, there was a cool breeze at the beach, and he knew it. True, he was nowhere near the beach, because she hated sand and water, but still he knew. There's always a cool breeze at the beach. They were in a cab coming back from somewhere, and he clutched the cardboard box wrapped in birthday paper the whole way. That present, in the cardboard box, was the biggest present he'd ever gotten. Not the most beautiful, but definitely the biggest. And he kept his arm around her the whole way, kissed her on the cheek, the breasts, more surprised with every kiss that she wasn't embarrassed. When he paid the fare, the ugly driver said he'd never seen a more perfect couple. He's on the road a lot, circling the city like a vulture over an open grave, but he's never seen a couple like them. And the second the driver said that, he felt this *heat* in his body. A buried heat that spreads only on the rare occasions when a great truth is in the air. And when he told her later, in bed, how he'd felt at that moment, she said that if he needed positive reinforcement from a pimple-faced cabdriver who couldn't even stay in his own lane, then their relationship must really be over. He pressed up against her and said she had such a nice heart and he loved it. She cried like a princess and said she wanted him to love her, all of her, not just her organs. Their eyes were closing now, and the sea breeze cooled his face as he fell asleep beside her, curled into himself like a child, like a baby.

IRONCLAD RULES

Usually, we don't kiss around other people. Cecile, with her plunging necklines and fuck-me shoes, is actually very shy. And I'm one of those guys who're always aware of every movement around them, who never manage to forget where they are. But it's a fact that on that morning, I did manage to forget, and we suddenly found ourselves, Cecile and me, hugging and kissing at a table in a coffeehouse like a pair of high-school kids trying to steal themselves a little intimacy in a public place.

When Cecile went to the bathroom, I finished my coffee in one gulp. I used the rest of the time to straighten out my clothes and my thoughts. "You're a lucky guy," I heard a voice with a thick Texas accent say from very close by. I turned my head. At the next table sat an older guy wearing a baseball cap. The whole time we were kissing, he was sitting practically on top of us, and we'd been rubbing and moaning into his bacon and eggs without even noticing. It was very embarrassing, but there was no way of apologizing without making it worse. So I gave him a sheepish smile and nodded.

"No, really," the old guy went on. "It's rare to hold on to that after you're married. A lot of people get hitched and it just disappears." "Like you said," I said, and kept on smiling, "I'm a lucky guy." "Me too," the old guy said, laughing, and raised his hand in the air, to show me his wedding band. "Me too. Forty-two years we're together, and it isn't even starting to get boring. You know, in my work, I have to fly a lot, and every time I leave her, let me tell you, I just feel like crying." "Forty-two years." I gave a long, polite whistle. "She must really be something." "Yes." The old guy nodded. I could see that he was trying to make up his mind whether to pull out a picture or not, and I was relieved when he gave up on the idea. It was getting more embarrassing by the minute, even though he obviously meant well. "I have three rules," the old guy said, smiling. "Three ironclad rules that help me keep it alive. You want to hear them?" "Sure," I said, gesturing at the waitress for more coffee. "One—" the old guy said, waving a finger in the air, "every day I try to find one new thing I love about her, even the smallest thing, you know, the way she answers the phone, how her voice rises when she's pretending she doesn't know what I'm talking about, things like that." "Every day?" I said. "That must really be hard." "Not that hard." The old guy laughed. "Not after you get the hang of it. The second rule—every time I see the children, and now the grandchildren too, I say to myself that half of my love for them is actually for her. Because half of them is her. And the last rule"—he continued as Cecile, who'd come back from the bathroom, sat down next to me—"when I come back from a trip, I always bring my wife a present. Even if I only go for a day." I nodded again and promised to remember. Cecile looked at us a little confused; after all, I wasn't exactly the kind of person who starts conversations with people in public places, and the old guy, who'd probably figured that out, got up to leave. He touched his hat and said to me, "Keep it up." And then he gave Cecile a small bow and left. "'My wife'?" Cecile said, grinning, and made a face. "'Keep it up'?" "It was nothing," I said, stroking her hand. "He saw my wedding band." "Ah," Cecile said, and kissed me on the cheek. "He looked a little weird."

On the flight back home, I sat alone, three seats all to myself, but as usual, I couldn't fall asleep. I was thinking about the deal with the Swiss company, which I didn't actually think would get off the ground, and about that PlayStation I bought for Roy, with the cordless joystick and everything. And when I thought about Roy, I kept trying to remember that half of my love for him is actually for Mira, and then I tried to think about one small thing I love about her—her expression, trying to stay cool, when she catches me in a lie. I even bought her a present from the duty-free cart on the plane, a new French perfume, which the smiling young flight attendant said everyone was wearing now. Even her. "Tell me," the flight attendant said, extending the back of her bronzed hand in my direction, "isn't that a fantastic scent?" It was true, her hand smelled great.

A GOOD-LOOKING
COUPLE

have nothing to lose, the girl thought, helping him unfasten her bra with one hand, leaning on the doorframe with the other. If he's a lousy fuck, I can at least say I had a lousy fuck, and if he's a great fuck, all the better, I'll enjoy it, plus I'll be able to say I had a great fuck, or if he's a dick to me afterward, I can say he was a lousy fuck just to get back at him.

I have nothing to lose, the guy thought. If she's a good fuck, I lucked out, and if she gives me a blow job, that's even better—but even if she's a lousy fuck, she's still one more girl. The twenty-second. The twenty-third, actually, if you count a hand job.

Something's going on, the cat thought, people coming in, bumping into furniture, making a racket, it's that kind of night. A lot of noise, but no milk for a long time, and hardly any food in the bowl, and even the little bit that's left is gross. That cat on the empty can might be smiling, but me, after licking the inside, I know he has nothing to smile about.

I have a good feeling about this, the girl thought. He's got a nice touch, kind of soft. Maybe this really is the beginning of something, maybe this is love. It's hard to know about things like that. I once had someone like him who turned into a real affair, but even that bombed out in the end. He was nice, but egocentric. Mostly nice to himself.

I have a good feeling about this, the guy thought. If we got this far, she probably won't stop in the middle, even though, who knows, I've met a few of those too. And then those impossible conversations. Sitting for hours in the living room. When you get into that sincerity routine, like there's something really deep going on. On the other hand, even that's better than the alternative. Especially when the alternative's eating baked beans in front of the TV.

I've had it, the TV thought. I've had it with how they turn me on and then leave the room, with how they sit in front of me but don't really watch. If they'd only take the trouble, they'd find out that I have so much to offer, a lot more than sports and videos and news, but for that, they have to dig a little deeper. And they stare at me like I was some piece of ass; if there's a cool video or some goal on the scoreboard, then great. If not, they're gone.

It's cold, the cat thought, too cold. Three weeks ago there was still sun. I'd sit outside on the air conditioner, happy as a king, and now I'm freezing, and them, they're warming each other up, having a ball. What do they care if it's cold here at night, and during the day, nothing but noise, and soot. Personally, I've had it with this country for a long time already.

Why am I always so cynical? the girl thought. Why do I have to keep thinking all the time instead of enjoying myself, looking at him through the slits of my eyes, and all I care about is what he thinks of me?

Wait, better not come too fast, the guy thought. It's not as good, plus it's lame, and she looks like the type who'll go and talk about it if you piss her off. I once heard there were techniques, maybe if I try to enjoy it less, maybe if I kind of zone out, it'll take longer.

He locked me, the door thought. Twice. From the inside. Most of the time he leaves me open. Maybe it's the visitor. Maybe he locked me unconsciously because in his heart he wanted her to stay. She actually looks like a nice person, a little sad, a little leery, but nice. The kind that, if you just uncover the manhole, everything inside is full of honey.

I'd get up to go to the bathroom, the girl thought, but I'm scared. The floor looks kind of sticky. A guy's apartment, what can you do? And if I start getting dressed now just for those few steps, I'll look insane or retarded. That's the last thing I need.

I could really be somebody, the guy thought, somebody great, a winner. I have things to say, but somehow, I can't manage to say them.

Maybe she's the one who'll understand.

I think I'll meow now, the cat thought. What do I have to lose, maybe they'll notice me, pet me a little, fill the bowl with milk. Lots of times girls like cats. I know, from experience.

What a good-looking couple, the door thought. I'd really be happy if something came of it and they moved in together. This place could definitely use a woman's touch.

I was uptight for no reason, the woman thought, the floor's even cleaner than mine, and the bathroom too. And his eyes, they're good eyes, and he kept holding me even after he came. I don't know if anything'll come of it. But even if it ends here, it was nice.

Maybe if I played an instrument, the man thought, if I'd stuck to it when I was a kid. Sometimes, there are these melodies in my head. It's so cute, the way she walks, tiptoeing, like she's afraid the floor's dirty. It's a good thing the maid was here on Friday.

A good program's starting on me now, the TV thought, now, of all times, when there's no one to watch. It pisses me off. Worse than pisses me off. If I wasn't on mute, I'd scream.

ANGLE

There's no telling why the three of them called it snooker when the game is actually called pool. But after all it isn't the name that counts, it's the pastime. And this way they could meet every day by the billiard table at the café, set up some kind of mini-tournament and feel like they were doing something. Most of the time, they were pretty evenly matched, because the only one who had a little experience, on account of growing up in the projects, had no coordination. The second guy may have had coordination, he just wasn't really motivated. And the third one, who was motivated as hell, never had an angle. Which meant that every time it was his turn, his shot was so impossible that he didn't stand a chance, even in theory.

Pool is a game for two, so that one of them would always have to sit it out, drinking coffee and talking on his cell phone. The one who'd grown up in the projects would call his girlfriend and talk baby talk to her, rubbing his finger around the plastic part you speak into as if he was stroking her lips. It's amazing how people can sound like retards when they're talking to their girlfriend, especially if they really love her a lot. Because when you're just fucking someone you make a point of keeping your cool, but when you're really in love—it can sound pretty repulsive. Speaking of fucking, the other guy, the one with the good coordination, he never took a latté, just a short and mean espresso, and meanwhile he'd be trying to navigate between all the calls from girls he'd come on to in the past week, putting one on hold, talking to another and so on. And he put so much effort into making sure none of the relationships he was juggling got too serious, that none of them ever did. Which sometimes from a distance seemed kind of sad.

And the third guy, the motivated one, was the only one who didn't order anything, and hardly ever used his phone, that's how immersed he was in the game. Once he even tried to make a rule that whenever they played, they would switch off their phones, but the others refused, which was sort of frustrating, because they were so busy yammering they never really paid attention to the game. Sitting on the side, instead of drinking and talking, he spent most of his time hating himself for losing the previous round. And somehow, it was always the same story, that when it came time for the critical shot, he didn't have an angle. The truth is that he didn't often sit it out, because he was so into it that whenever he had a miss, he'd start to cheat. And the others would almost always let him get away with it, because when you drag it out with the same girlfriend for three years, or when there are four chicks that you're feeling bad about, all at the same time, then losing a game of snooker starts to seem like small change. So that on paper, everything should just have kept going. Except that the motivated guy knew in his heart that if he wanted to win, he'd have to keep cheating, and that he was cheating his best buddies. And it bothered him, because deep down inside he was a very honest guy. And he was so set on finding a different solution that he'd stay behind every day after his buddies left, and practice, trying to figure out what he was doing wrong. From the side, it looked sort of pathetic: a bald thirty-two-year-old kid racking up the balls, shooting with the tip of the cue, and cursing himself almost voicelessly every time he missed.

It went on that way for many days till the waitress who worked there decided to help him out. She taught him one simple trick: always, a tenth of a second before he shoots, he should stop thinking about the shot, and think about something else instead, something nice. To his surprise, this trick almost always worked, and suddenly he became so good that his friends didn't want to play with him anymore. They both said that was why, but the truth was there were other reasons. The guy from the projects was about to become a father, and he was busy all the time with ultrasounds and mortgages and all kinds of Lamaze courses. And the other guy had so many girls and bad scenes on his mind that he couldn't concentrate long enough to hold the cue straight. So the only thing left for the motivated guy to do was to play against the waitress. And even though she'd beat him all the time, he didn't really care anymore. This waitress was called Karen, and she had one ironclad rule—not to date customers, but because the motivated guy never ordered anything, she didn't really consider him a customer, so at least in theory he stood a chance.

HIMME

At age thirty-one, Himme found that almost all the dreams the people closest to him ever had for him were coming true:

He'd succeeded no less than everyone had expected him to, but he remained modest, which made his father proud. Not to mention the fact that he had married just the way his parents and his wife had always dreamed he would. He even had his health, except for that minor business with the hemorrhoids. And yet, Himme wasn't happy—which often made him feel frustrated. His mother, after all, ever since he was a little boy, had always wanted him to be happy.

SOMETHING EXCITING

If Himme could have wished for anything, what would he have wished for?

Quiet? Quiet is serenity, it's a bubble bath, it's grass growing, it's what happens in your refrigerator after you close the door and the little light goes out. In short, quiet is nothingness. And we'll have more than enough of that nothingness eventually, definitely, once we die. For now, Himme felt, what was needed here was something entirely different. Something, never mind what it was called as long as it tugged at his heart, like a whale song. Something strong, something tough and dangerous, but something that would end in success. Something that would fill his soul to the brim, causing it to overflow, yet could be contained. Something exciting, but really exciting, like love, or a mission, or an idea that would take the world light-years forward. Something like that was just what he needed. At least one, preferably two, urgently. Because the guy's dying here in the meantime. And the situation, despite his apparent nonchalance, was really and truly serious. "I heard Suzanne Vega's coming to town," his wife said, without looking up from the paper. "How about it?" "Why not?" he said, and wiped the sweat from his face, trying not to let her see how agitated he was. "Her first record I really liked," she said. "The second one not as much, and the third I haven't heard, but everyone says it's lousy. And they say she's got a book out that you can only order online. We could get tickets. Yael too. I'm sure she'd love to come."

Yael was a good friend of his wife's. Not very pretty, not terribly interesting. But with a very smooth complexion and the enticing smell of an easy lay. Once, before he got married, he'd fantasize about that kind of girl, half jerking off, half praying for one to show up. Actually, completely jerking off and completely praying. Not that it did him much good. And today, married and faithful, it really didn't matter anymore.

"Whatever you want, honey," he said, stressing the *you* almost abjectly.

The tickets were expensive, and the show kind of dull, but moving too. She looked sad when she sang, and it really tugged at Himme's heart. At one point he imagined himself going up on stage and kissing her. An electrifying kiss that would make her his, right then and there. Then she gave an encore. But even though they gave her a standing ovation, she didn't come out for another number. She went back to America. Maybe suicide, he thought to himself that same night as he tried to maneuver without spilling the drinks he'd gotten for his wife and Yael. Yeah, maybe suicide.

A BROKEN HEART

He actually had a relationship once with someone who'd committed suicide. Not emotional, physical. It happened in the army. He was serving in general-staff headquarters at the time, and he'd been brought up on charges of being seen with his boots unpolished. And just when he was walking past the tall staff headquarters building, someone dropped to the ground next to him, splattered. A girl-soldier, they said, with a broken heart, a corporal, Liat Something. Later he remembered hearing a kind of scream above him as she was falling. But he hadn't looked up. The sound didn't even register.

He reached the hearing all covered in her blood. They let him off. Liat Atlas. That was her name. They even called on him later, to testify at the military police investigation. It couldn't go on this way, that much he knew. Maybe he needed therapy.

LOTS OF PATIENCE

Himme's therapist was hairy.

Himme's therapist took tons of money.

Himme's therapist said it takes lots and lots of patience.

Most of the time he just listened.

When he did say something, it was usually something dumb, or an annoying question.

It takes lots and lots of patience.

Once he told his therapist: "Enough about me—let's talk about you." And Himme's therapist gave him the tired smile of someone who'd heard that crack more than once, but under the smile it was also obvious that he didn't have much to tell. From the look of it, the only thing working in the therapist's favor was the exhausting allure of mystery. Mystery. Like between a guy and a girl on their first date, that uncertainty, will he try to kiss her, will she agree, and if she does, what will her body look like naked? Mystery was the only card his therapist had up his sleeve, and he wasn't about to give it up so easily.

At that session, neither of them said anything for fifty minutes. Himme spent those fifty minutes thinking about what if his therapist had been a beautiful, voluptuous woman and Himme got up out of his chair and kissed her long, smooth neck. How would she react? A slap? Maybe a half-surprised moan? Except that his therapist wasn't a beautiful, voluptuous woman. "It takes lots of patience," he told Himme at the end of that session, as he filled in the invoice, "lots of patience." And they both opened their datebooks and made believe they were really going to meet again.

SCIENCE FICTION

Once he read an interview with a marriage counselor, who said that in order to rekindle their relationship a couple should clean the bathtub together in the nude, or buy special underwear made of sugar and lick it off each other until it dissolved. Himme and his wife never did things like the complicated ideas he read about in the paper, but still it was obvious that after a very tired half-year they were suddenly onto something. Like in those futuristic movies, where they always have those weapons that track a person's frequency, and the person starts resonating until the special effects come on and everything explodes somehow, he and his wife succeeded in finding some secret frequency in each other too. "Why don't we go abroad," his wife purred after one of the times when he came. "We've never fucked abroad." "We fucked in Sinai," he said. "Sinai doesn't count. It's Egypt," she said, drawing close to him, and kissed him on the eyes. "Let's go somewhere overseas. Let's go to Greece."

HERE

In the end, they didn't go to Greece. They tried, but it didn't work out—and it was because of her. His job had a special offer on an Internet linkup, and he tried for hours to log on. When he succeeded, he spent most of his time looking for the names of people he'd known, from work and from life. Once, on the Web site of some Dutch anarchist DJs, he found the name of his upstairs neighbor, or maybe it was a different Stanislav Hershko. His own name he couldn't find anywhere, but he discovered soon enough how to outsmart the system, and slip it into some sites, and ever since then he'd visited so many of them, that on his most recent search for his name he'd received seventy hits. "I've got to get out of here," he thought, but he also knew that as long as he wasn't able to figure out where *here* was, he didn't stand a chance.

COMPLETELY ALONE

One night he had a dream that was almost prophetic. In the dream, he was in a faraway country, sitting naked on the sidewalk. In his dream, he wasn't quite sure what he was doing there. He looked down at his feet to see if there was any money on the ground. If there had been any, even a single coin, he could have thought he was a beggar. Except that there was nothing. Which

made Himme think that maybe in the dream he was an unsuc-
cessful beggar or maybe even a street performer. Strange, whenever he dreamed, the thing that interested him most was his
profession. Even in his most abstract dreams, the kind where you
lose all your teeth, or where you're drowning, his first thought
was always: "Am I a drowning captain? A naval officer on a mis-
sile ship? Maybe a fisherman?" And as he was being swooped up
into the whirlpool of his dream, he'd keep struggling, trying to reconstruct, by the items of clothing, what his elusive profession
might be. Except that in this dream, where he'd been sitting completely naked on the sidewalk, it was obvious that his profession
was not the issue. The fact that he was naked was no big deal either. The point about this dream was somewhere altogether different, somewhere that couldn't be referred to by name. The man
who was him in the dream was feeling things that couldn't even
be put into words, and the real Himme, the one who'd been a visitor in the dream and had only been thinking about professions,
was kind of embarrassed that he couldn't be more like him.
Strange, Himme thought, to be jealous of your own self in your
own dream. And for what? For being naked? For sitting on the
sidewalk? For being completely alone?

OTHER THOUGHTS

In the end she left him. It was odd. He'd been having thoughts for
such a long time that if she'd only known about them, she'd have
been sobbing her heart out, or slapping him, or both, and all that
time, while he was looking at her to see if she could tell, Himme's
wife was having thoughts of her own. From where he was sitting,
they *looked* totally innocent: thoughts about cakes and desserts,
vacations, a spa, her mother's health. But in the end, it turned out

that she'd been having other thoughts too, thoughts that made her leave him. Never mind leave. Divorce him. If they'd had a kid, they'd probably have figured out a solution or at least they'd have kept trying, for the kid's sake. But this way, without a kid, there wasn't even anyone to make the effort for.

NISSIM

In the evening, two days after Himme's wife left, there was a hesitant knock at the door. Nonchalantly Himme went to see who it was, trying not to show any happiness or hope as he opened the door without checking through the peephole first. Standing in the doorway were Nissim Roman and his little daughter, Fortuna, their arms full of dairy products. "Our fridge broke down all of a sudden," Nissim Roman said shyly. "It's a crappy fridge. When the repairman comes in the morning, I'll give him hell. And I thought that maybe in the meantime, if there's room, we could keep a few things in yours." When Himme opened his fridge for them, Nissim tried not to show how sorry he felt for him. "Lots of room," he said, giving Himme an embarrassed smile, and Fortuna arranged the dairy products on one of the empty shelves in neat little stacks. "We'll take them tomorrow," Nissim promised, "bright and early," and he and Fortuna went home, leaving Himme alone with himself.

All night long, Himme couldn't fall asleep. And whenever he did, he dreamed how he was stealing into the fridge and drinking the buttermilk that belonged to Nissim Roman and his sad-eyed daughter, and he'd wake up alarmed. There was something scary about his craving for that buttermilk. Something very scary. The next morning, the little girl came and took everything. Only then did Himme manage to fall asleep. Five minutes later his father phoned, and woke him up.

THE OLD GUARD

If there was one thing that Himme's dad was really good at it was writing eulogies. He had that special knack for pinpointing in the dead the qualities that would make us miss them. When he was young, Himme's dad hadn't had many opportunities to exercise this extraordinary talent of his. But now that he and his friends had passed seventy, he had his hands full. "Velvaleh died yesterday," he told Himme on the phone. "Your mother hated him, you know, and it's her canasta night besides, so she's not coming. Could you come to the funeral with me by any chance?" Which is how Himme found himself at the cemetery in ninety-degree heat at the open grave of another one of the people his father used to call the Old Guard, listening to an insecure, awkward rabbi produce all sorts of weird mumblings and waiting patiently for his father to inspire him and the others, the way he always did, with a sense of loss and sorrow. Except that in the case of Velvaleh, Himme was sad to begin with, so it was a slam dunk. Himme tried to recall Velvaleh's facial features, which he'd known since childhood, but he didn't do very well. What he did remember, down to the last detail, was his amazing ability to look like just about every other person you've ever known. Every time Himme met him in the street, he'd be sure it was Pinchas, one of his dad's other friends, or Mr. Pliskin, who used to own a grocery store on Bialik Street, or any number of other people. Even Himme's dad would always get mixed up. Everyone did. Women who wanted to flatter Velvaleh would tell him he reminded them of some movie star, and the truth was that—whatever star you picked—he did remind you of him, kind of. Beside the open grave Himme's dad said that Velvaleh had grown so used to being mistaken for other people, that when he heard someone call out a name in the street, any name, he'd always turn around, because he knew they were really calling him. "Once, when we were sitting at Café Aviv," Himme's dad eulogized, eyes moist, "Velvaleh asked me if I thought all those people made the same mistake in the other direction too, and called out 'Velvaleh! Velvaleh!' in the street when they saw somebody else."

A HOUSE WITHOUT ROACHES

Nissim Roman and his little daughter were standing there, in the backyard of his building, staring, transfixed, at a man in a T-shirt that read "The Eichmann of Roaches." It had a picture underneath of a giant roach floundering, on its back. The exterminator was trying to lift the drain cover and went on telling the Romans how the chief entomologist of the Ministry of Health had once told him there was no such thing as a house without roaches. The roaches are always there, but because they only come out in the dark you don't notice them living right next to you. And by the time you notice them, even if it's just one or two, it means you've got lots more where those came from. And sure enough, right under the cover, there were like a million roaches scurrying in all directions. "Yikes!" little Fortuna shrieked, and ran away, and Nissim Roman scrambled after her in his flip-flops. The only ones left in the yard now were the exterminator, a terrified swarm of roaches in their death throes, and Himme, sweating away in the drab suit his dad had insisted on lending him. The exterminator stopped spraying the sewer for a moment and pointed at Himme's head. "From one funeral to the next, eh?" That's when Himme realized he was still wearing the cardboard yarmulke they gave him at the cemetery.

TEN TIMES MORE

Once or twice a day, Himme would snoop on his ex-wife, peeking into her new apartment from up in one of the trees across the street. Most of the time, she wasn't doing anything special. Just the kind of stuff he knew about from when they were married: TV, lots of books, watching a movie with Yael. After her shower, she'd stare at her figure in the mirror, pinching herself all over, and making cute faces. The truth was that it was very easy to like her during this ceremony, and Himme wondered if this was something new or maybe she'd always done it but he just hadn't noticed, because he'd only started snooping on her after they broke up. Maybe, he thought, there are lots of things about her that I don't know, and if I'd known about those things when we were still married, I'd have loved her ten times more. And me too, maybe there are a million cute things like that about me, and if she'd known about them, she'd never have wanted to leave me. Who knows—maybe lots of nice things had passed between them, coming out in the dark, like the roaches, and just because they'd gone unnoticed, it didn't mean they hadn't been there, nevertheless.

SALES TAX

"Think about it," Himme's dad said once. "I've never been to In-dia, and you've always wanted to go. Your mother said she'd be glad to have a break from me for a few weeks too. What do you say?" And when he saw Himme hesitate, he continued: "Look, me, my life is over. All I have left now is the sales tax. No real commitments, no real worries, just a couple of short espressos, some quality time with my darling son, and maybe, if we can fit it in, an elephant trek. And you too, son, what have you got to do around here anyway? How much longer can you keep peeping at your ex-wife in the shower? Sooner or later they'll arrest you, or else you'll fall out of the tree. Wouldn't it be better to spend some time with your dad—to visit one of the Seven Wonders of the World with your dad?"

INDIA

The revolving restaurant on the rooftop of their Delhi hotel had one song, Frank Sinatra's "My Way," on a continuous loop. Over and over again, at every meal, "My Way," three meals a day. For Himme, the cumulative effect of the cumulative listening to the cumulative song was cumulatively distressing. Himme's dad took it in his stride, and even kept whistling along with Sinatra over and over, but Himme refused to resign himself to this fate, and on their third day he demanded an explanation. He took it up with the manager: "Why the same song?" The smiling manager wobbled his head slowly in the Indian manner: "This is like asking why the same restaurant turns around and around. The restaurant is turning around and around because this is the best restaurant in Delhi. Same with the song. 'My Way' is the best song, and in the best restaurant in Delhi we are playing only the best." "Yes, but there are other songs. Also good songs," Himme attempted.

"'My Way' is the best song," the manager said, repeating his mantra with smiling resolve. "No second best for my guests."

RAMAT GAN

The world outside the revolving restaurant seemed even stranger, and Himme found himself sticking to the hotel room, while his father made valiant sorties into the outside world and came back armed with new experiences and leprosy-stricken friends, who

were glad to join him in the elevator to the fourteenth floor in order to meet his very talented, albeit somewhat depressive, son.

When he felt he'd exhausted Delhi, Himme's dad dragged his
plaintive son northward, to breathtakingly beautiful villages,
where even Himme began to enjoy himself. The beauty and the
generosity and openness of the Indians along with Himme's dad's
Old Guard stories all came together in his mind, in an overwhelming but incredibly moving jumble. And so, riding an elephant at sunset, he heard the sad life story of the meticulously
well-mannered boxer who'd come to Ramat Gan all the way
from Freiburg, Germany, and established the Atom Bar from
scratch, learning how, with a single terrible left hook and half a
heart he'd knocked down both Sinkevitch brothers, even though
deep down inside him he believed that knocking down clients
would be bad luck, and indeed three years later the bar was
burned to the ground by a tattooed Maori gentile after a local
hooker insulted him.

As it turned out, the Indians loved Himme's dad's stories too.
They listened very closely, and usually laughed in the right places,
which sometimes helped Himme forget that they hadn't understood a word. A closer study revealed that rather than listening,
they were actually concentrating on his dad's glorious bare potbelly, and the way it shimmied whenever he described something
particularly funny or moving. On the underside of his dad's belly
there was a scar from when he'd had his appendix out, and one
of the Indians told Himme in broken English that every time the
scar turned red, they knew the story had taken a very dangerous
turn. Himme's dad took his swelling audience in stride, and kept
on reminiscing out loud, even as he swallowed the saliva that
filled his mouth while he carried on about Shiyya Barbalat,
the legendary wandering junkman from Hamavdil Street, who'd
snuck around town with his horse and carriage one night, and

beheaded all the "No Horses Allowed" signs, then scattered their ravaged carcasses in the backyard of the municipal department of motor vehicles. It was an interesting question what the Indians would think if they could actually understand. They would probably imagine this Ramat Gan as an exotic place. And even to Himme, who'd grown up on Hashalom Road, not quite a mile from where all the stories took place, his dad's Ramat Gan sounded like something far away—not just in space and in time, but also in a million other dimensions that he couldn't even name.

LIKE HIMSELF

Himme's dad's death came out of nowhere. Suddenly his dad was feeling "under the weather," suddenly a dizziness, suddenly a fever, suddenly they needed a doctor but there wasn't a doctor to be found. Drink a lot, stay in the room, and rest. Himme's dad kept smiling the whole time. The fever, he'd tell Himme, felt sort of good. "It's like after a bottle of rye," he'd say, laughing, "only without the upset stomach." When he and Himme were alone, it seemed like nothing, but judging by the concern of the Indian who was renting them the room, it was obviously serious. Himme's dad was calm, and he wasn't just pretending to be calm, but that didn't really say anything about the situation. It wasn't about dying, after all, just about getting a sales-tax rebate. His real life had been over for a while anyway. All the rest was an add-on, a kind of quality adventure with his darling son on the wide tax bracket of time.

After he died, Himme buried him in the backyard of the house where they were staying. The Indian landlord tried to persuade him it would be better to have the body cremated, but when he saw that Himme was adamant, he got some spades and dug along beside him. By the time they'd finished covering the grave, it was evening, and Himme was busy taking care of a blister that had developed on the thumb of his digging hand, and wondering what to inscribe on the tombstone. It was strange how his dad had been so good at eulogies, and here Himme couldn't come up with a single sentence. The only thing that occurred to him in connection with his dad was that he was utterly like himself. Lots of thoughts got mixed up together in his head, that it had been a mistake to bury his father there, and that he should have taken the body back home, and that he ought to call right away, call his mother, whom he was missing a lot, and maybe his ex-wife too, who had loved Himme's dad very much, that maybe this sad situation would cause her to come back to him, at least for a short while, out of pity. Other thoughts had to do with Barbalat, with Velvaleh, with the Atom Bar, with that whole world that Himme had never known, a world with which Himme's dad had been at one. And thoughts about passports and rupees presented themselves too, and thoughts about what on earth would happen next and another tiny glimpse—of how life had protected him until now, like a Fabergé egg in a padded box, and of how in his entire thirty-two years the world had hardly confronted him with anyone who'd died (two people): his dad, and the girl-soldier with the broken heart who'd fallen to the ground beside him at staff headquarters. He sat and waited for all those thoughts to pass, but when he realized they were just going on and on, he got up, stuck a piece of wood in the mound, took a black felt-tip pen, and printed THE OLD GUARD in large bold letters.

FORTUNA

Even after Himme's dad died, Himme kept on roaming around India with no particular goal in mind. Some of the time he felt bored or shitty, for no reason. Lots of times he felt happiness, for no especially good reason either. In one small town, not far from Aurangabad, he met an Indian girl who looked exactly like his neighbor's daughter, Fortuna. She was playing hopscotch with another little girl, slightly older, and just like Fortuna Roman, the Indian Fortuna remained serious all during the game, and even when she won, her eyes stayed sad. After the game he followed her home, and saw that the Indian Fortuna also lived in an apartment, half a floor up on the left. Because he'd kept his distance as he followed her, he couldn't see who opened the door when she rang the bell. The voice of whoever opened it spoke Hindi, but it sounded surprisingly like Nissim Roman. Which meant that the apartment opposite theirs might just belong to the Indian Himme. And Himme was terribly eager to knock on his door, but he didn't have the nerve.

He sat on the stairs and tried to imagine what life must be like for the Indian Himme behind that door. And wondered how much like him he really was. Whether he was divorced, whether his father was alive, whether his father had stories about Aurangabad of earlier days too, and whether his wife's Indian girlfriend also had the smell of an easy lay. Three hours later, the door opened and out came a grim young Indian with a handlebar mustache. He looked at Himme and Himme looked at him and neither one lowered his gaze. After a few seconds, Himme was feeling so uneasy that he got up and left. Deep in his heart, he hoped that the sad Indian was nothing like him at all.

NO ATTACHMENT

The whole time Himme was wandering aimlessly, he didn't once phone his mother back home, and it made him feel guilty and mean. He didn't phone his ex-wife either, or anyone else for that matter. All in all, he didn't do much talking to people in India, and he spent most of his time on his own. Until he reached the guest house in Puna, where a group of three Israeli sannyasis started talking to him in Hebrew about Existence, against his will. The most talkative of the lot was called Bashir. Sometimes the other sannyasis called him Moshe, but he'd correct them. Bashir told Himme that you could tell at a glance he was far from his center, and that this was very sad, because Bashir had also been far from his center once, and he'd studied at the College of Business Administration, and only now, in retrospect, when he'd found half the light, did he understand how terribly he'd been suffering. Himme tried to pretend in English that he didn't understand what Bashir was saying and that he was really a tourist from Italy, but his accent was a giveaway. "Man," Bashir said, placing his hand on Himme's shoulder, "you've got to be more trusting. You need to get in touch with yourself. Don't you realize what's happening to you? You're in a very bad head." And Himme, who really was not in touch with what was happening to him, and with what it meant to be in a very bad head, moved even further away from his center and tried to sock Bashir in the jaw, but he missed, and slipped, and banged his head against the edge of the table, just at the very moment when the three sannyasis spotted two German girls and rushed over to offer them a tantric relationship with no attachment, which would help them connect to their true selves.

FLIP

The truth is that Moshe, or Bashir, or whatever his name was, had a point, and Himme really was in a terrible head. He was angry, and he was bored, and he was homesick, and he was so much of all of those that he thought he was going to explode. He felt like a victim, he felt guilty, he felt upstanding, he felt that he had no name, and even more than he was feeling, he was thinking.

A typical thought by way of example: at night, when we say we're going to sleep, and we get into bed and shut our eyes, we're not really asleep. We're just pretending. We shut our eyes and breathe rhythmically, pretending to be asleep, until the deceit grows slowly real. And maybe that's how it is with death. Himme's dad hadn't died right away either. And the whole time when his eyes were shut and he wasn't moving, you could still feel his pulse. Maybe Himme's dad had been dying just like someone going to sleep—pretending, until it became real. And if so, then it was altogether possible that if only Himme had interrupted him in the process, jumped on his bed like a little kid, opened one of his eyes to make sure, shouted "Dad!" and tickled him— the whole deceit would simply have fallen apart.

GRACIA

Himme returned to his room, his forehead bleeding. He didn't have a first-aid kit, and he didn't really feel like looking for the owner of the guest house and asking whether he had one. Near the door to his room, he bumped into a tourist who struck him as oddly familiar. She told him in broken English that she was French, and that she'd be glad to lend him a bandage. He told her he was Italian, and even added "Gracia" at the end. But both of them knew for sure that they were Israelis who were tired of meeting other Israelis in the East. So she helped him with the bandage, in English, and he smiled at her, and tried to remember where he knew her from. In the end, without either of them really planning it, they went to bed. And afterward, when they'd already told each other their real names, he figured it out. "Sivan Atlas?" he said, with a lopsided smile. "I think I met your sister, but only once and just for a second, may she rest in peace."

At night Sivan cried, and at least from the outside it seemed to be helping her feel better, and so did Himme. He let go of his tears the way a hot-air balloon jettisons another extra-heavy bag of sand, and as they lay there in each other's arms, he felt as though if only he'd let go of her, he'd start floating up toward the ceiling. The next morning, Sivan continued to Dharamsala according to plan, and Himme, who didn't have one, remained.

ONE SERIOUS MIND-FUCK

He lit himself a cigarette. Until recently he'd still been trying to quit, but by now he'd seen enough of the light to understand it didn't really matter. "I don't suppose you have another one for me?" asked his baba, who was a helpless miser and basically an ass-hole. "No," he lied. "It's my last one." A particularly good-looking Dutch trekker stopped beside them, looking for a hostel. And the baba gave her some vague reply about how the whole world is really one big hostel, and managed, as if just in passing, to hit her up for an unfiltered Lucky Strike and a pack of sugarless gum. He also tried to work up a conversation, but when he saw she wasn't interested, he reverted to spirituality. "Beautiful, eh?" the baba asked, smiling at him. "Sure." Himme nodded. "But what difference does it make, Baba? I don't really exist anyway, do I?" "You'd make it with her, wouldn't you?" the baba sniggered, and took a drag on his Lucky Strike. "How can I make it with her if I don't really exist?" he shot back. "If she doesn't really exist? Believe me, this whole existence thing is just one serious mind-fuck. You're a baba. You of all people should know what I mean." "I'd screw her brains out," the baba persisted, not listening. Strange, that of all the babas that Shiva had scattered around the world, Himme had to go and choose the only one who also happened to drive a cab. Countless roads lead to enlightenment. Buddha, for example, reached Nirvana through despair; Chang-Chu, through inaction. It would be interesting to find out what his baba's road was. Reality grew sharper around him, deionizing itself of every bit of dirt or haziness, as he began to sink into a state of no-mind. "I need some more money, for dahl," the baba said, nudging him gently till he responded, and then returned to eat it next to him, taking care not to get his clothes dirty. "Where do you think that Dutch chick went?" he asked with his mouth full. "She didn't really exist," Himme insisted. "She was just a thought." And the baba, who'd become thirsty again, borrowed some money from him for a Coke. "Once," he said, "I got laid by some tourist. Nothing great, kind of fat. But she kept laughing the whole time. I love it when girls laugh." Himme felt everything around him fading away, like an old thought, like a half-forgotten memory. "I'll be back in a minute," the baba said. "I just want to look into something." And even though he knew that time was just an illusion, Himme nodded. "If you give me a little cash, I'll buy us some cigarettes," the baba said, and started playing around with the sole of his shoe. "Look at my shoes, they're full of holes. So how about that Dutch babe, didn't she seem interested?" While the baba was off buying cigarettes, Buddha arrived to visit him, smiling and chubby as always, with the tip of a familiar scar showing on the underside of his potbelly, and Buddha even brought him a present—a wicker basket full of dandelions gone to seed. He blew on one of the dandelions, and the whole world disappeared.